Mike Richardson, Roy Watling

Keys to Fungi on Dung

Mike Richardson, Roy Watling

Keys to Fungi on Dung

ISBN/EAN: 9783337626273

Printed in Europe, USA, Canada, Australia, Japan

Cover: Foto ©Andreas Hilbeck / pixelio.de

More available books at **www.hansebooks.com**

KEYS TO FUNGI
ON DUNG

by

M. J. RICHARDSON
165 Braid Road,
EDINBURGH EH10 6JE

and

ROY WATLING
Royal Botanic Garden,
EDINBURGH EH3 5LR

Published by the British Mycological Society
PO Box 30, Stourbridge
West Midlands DY9 9PZ

Printed in Scotland by BPC-AUP Aberdeen Ltd

ISBN 0 9527704 2 3

The first edition of these keys was published in the *Bulletin of the British Mycological Society* **2**, 18-43 (1968) and **3**, 86-88, 121-124 (1969) in an attempt to bring together in one place information for the identification of coprophilous fungi which would be useful to teachers and others interested in these fungi. They were issued as a separate publication in 1972, and with corrections in 1974. They were reprinted in 1982 with additions. This latest edition is an update of all the earlier ones, with current nomenclature and recent references, and the inclusion of some additional species.

M.J.R.
R.W.
December 1996

INTRODUCTION

Coprophilous fungi are highly satisfactory for demonstrating the diversity and morphology of a group of related organisms within an ecological system. Representative genera of most major groups of fungi can usually be guaranteed to appear on dung after a period of incubation. There is no shortage of dung in our fields and woods, and this material will always produce characteristic fungi at whatever time of year it is collected.

Dung is best incubated in a light place, for example on a table in a warm room, on layers of moist filter paper or other absorbent material. For rabbit pellets, and samples of similar size, Petri dishes are ideal; for horse 'apples', and larger types of dung, large covered dishes such as glass casseroles, plastic sandwich boxes or yoghurt pots are needed. The top third cut from a plastic lemonade or mineral water bottle fits neatly in a Petri dish, and replacing the screw cap with a cotton wool plug allows aeration and gives adequate height for developing basidiomycetes. Samples should not be kept in airtight containers for any length of time after collection, as in such conditions insects and nematodes tend to break down the dung, and anaerobic conditions which do not favour the fungi rapidly develop. If they cannot be set to incubate soon after collection they can be gently air dried, as most dung fungi will remain alive after such treatment and grow out when the sample is eventually moistened. The absorbent material should be kept moist. Although free water will not allow the best development of ascomycetes, the succession of basidiomycetes appears to vary with the wetness of the dung. Earthworms and insect larvae should be excluded from the samples as far as possible, for they break up the dung too much; activity of the latter can be reduced by spraying lightly with a household insecticide. If space is limited and cultures are kept nearby, it is very important to prevent mite infestation. Containers can be isolated by placing on glass plates lightly smeared with Vaseline, to which an acaricide (e.g. methyl benzoate) can be added.

Fungi are best sought with a stereoscopic binocular microscope, when their full beauty will be seen, but a hand lens or simple magnifier, although less convenient, is sufficient for all but the smallest forms. The larger ascomycetes and most of the basidiomycetes are readily seen with the unaided eye, but the binocular microscope is still very useful for observing the gross features of the veil of the basidiomycetes. Perithecia, apothecia and similar structures can be removed with fine needles or forceps quite cleanly for mounting, initially in water, on slides. Subsequent irrigation with iodine solution will allow any reaction of ascus wall, tip or pore to be observed, and mounting in diluted Indian ink can enhance the visibility of appendages, caudae and sheaths which occur on some spores. Spore discharge in the ascomycetes often occurs from mature asci when material is mounted in water, so mature spores can immediately be seen. Many of the coprophilous toadstools (agarics), because of their small size and/or rapidly deliquescent nature, often do not give spore prints in the normal way, but mature spores can usually be found on the stipe or in natural spore prints formed on the absorbent

5

material on which the dung is supported. For accurate identification the ability to measure the size of spores and other structures will be necessary. Basic microscopical technique and mycological knowledge is assumed. Common species are well described and illustrated in popular books, and references are given to specialist works to allow descriptions of less common species to be found. It will be necessary to refer to these for critical taxa. Although this edition contains about one half more species than the 1982 edition, there are still many species to be described and new records and observations to be made, especially in the Ascomycotina.

Four keys are presented. Keys 1 and 2 (MJR) are to the coprophilous ascomycetes, a very diverse group which, although not covering all the possible types of reproductive structure found in the class, contains many of the important types. The information for the identification of these fungi is dispersed throughout the literature, and many new species are still being discovered and described. Some appear to be world-wide in their distribution, others more restricted, with a prevalence of reports from either arctic, temperate or tropical regions. These keys are not exhaustive, since there are far too many species to make it practical to include them all. They do, however, include most genera, and the commoner or well known species of temperate regions. Specific (and even generic) limits in some cases (e.g. *Coprotus* / *Ascophanus* / *Ryparobius* / *Thelebolus*) are still the subject of debate and the choice of names to use in the key for a few taxa has been a compromise. Key 2 includes the original 'plectomycete' key (RW), which contains fungi which may not be strictly coprophilous in the normal sense, but fungi which occur on hair, horn, bone and cadavers, and may thus be found on carnivore dung or pellets of owls and other birds of prey.

Key 3 (RW, p. 52) is to the basidiomycetes of dung and associated debris. The part of the key dealing with the agarics attempts to be as complete as possible. Since the toadstools have always been thought of as the best known of the coprophilous fungi, attention to their taxonomy has often been careless. In this key the opportunity has been taken to adopt a rather narrow species concept, and to provide in certain places indications of where distinct taxa, even autonomous species, may be found after further laboratory work. Many of these types have been cultured and appear to differ vegetatively in ways which support observations of gross morphology. Coprophilous agarics are popular material for genetic studies and additional information on veil structure, spore number etc. of individual species is given, even when these are not 'key characters'.

Key 4 (MJR, p. 63) is to the Zygomycota (phycomycetes) which are characteristic of dung and amongst the first to appear when freshly dropped dung is incubated. They soon disappear, however, but their fruiting can be prolonged by plating small portions of dung on a nutrient medium (e.g. potato carrot or potato dextrose agar) to which has been added a small amount of antibiotic to reduce bacterial growth. This method is especially suitable for the parasitic and predacious fungi. A cultural approach is essential for the identification of many of these fungi and the above media, and oatmeal agar, are suitable for culture as well as isolation. For this reason the study of this group of fungi is less easy than that of the ascomycetes and basidiomycetes but, because the asexual stages are characteristic, we have attempted to key out the commoner genera which might be found, with notes on common species. The asexual spores are sporangiospores formed in sporangia; some sporangia produce a single spore within a closely fitting sporangium,

7

and have in the past been erroneously described as conidia. A great range of sporangial structure occurs within the orders concerned. The classical structure is the massive (up to 250μm diam.) multispored sporangium with an internal columella which remains after the spores have been dispersed (e.g. *Mucor*); those of *Mortierella* are similar, but smaller and without a columella. Other sporangia are much reduced and may be only 10-20μm diam., and contain only a small number of spores (*Thamnidium*) or one spore (*Chaetocladium*); these small globose structures are termed sporangioles. Spores may also form in chains; the chains are in terminal groups and are formed by the differentiation of the contents of cylindrical sporangia which are considered to be part-sporangia (merosporangia). When the sporangial wall has disappeared the spore chains may remain discrete and intact, or they may collapse into a wet droplet of spores (*Syncephalastrum*, some *Piptocephalis*). Members of the Kickxellaceae (e.g. *Coemansia*, *Kickxella*) have single spored merosporangia produced in serried ranks on boat-shaped or swollen structures (sporoclades). The sexual spores (zygospores) are rarely seen without culturing; oatmeal agar is one which favours their production. The key includes one member of the Entomophthorales, which also produces single-spored sporangia. Other members of this order may be found parasitising the various animals which live in dung; many other predacious fungi may also be seen, e.g. parasites of amoebae (*Acaulopage*). The key is of necessity far from complete, and omits members of the Dimargaritales, which have been found frequently on dung of small mammals in America.

Mitosporic fungi ('Fungi Imperfecti') and myxomycetes have been excluded, since they would expand the range of these keys beyond what was initially intended, although numerous species of both groups occur on dung when incubated in a damp chamber. For mitosporic fungi see Seifert, Kendrick & Murase (1983) and Ellis & Ellis (1988); for myxomycetes see Eliasson & Lundqvist (1979). As practical keys, rather than a taxonomic treatment, taxonomic authorities have not been cited. For ascomycetes, Cannon, Hawksworth & Sherwood-Pike (1985) have been followed, unless there is a more recent treatment of a group. For the basidiomycetes the 'New Checklist of British Agarics and Boleti' (Dennis, Orton & Hora, 1960, *Supplement to the Transactions of the British Mycological Society* **43**) has been followed, and *The British Fungus Flora* (Orton & Watling, 1979 and Watling, 1982).

ASCOMYCETE REFERENCES

Ahmed, S. I. & Cain, R. F. (1972). Revision of the genera *Sporormia* and *Sporormiella*. *Canadian Journal of Botany* **50**, 419-477. (Keys and descriptions of 66 spp.).

Apinis, A. E. (1964). Revision of the British Gymnoascaceae. *Mycological Paper* **96**.

Arx, J. A. von (1971). On *Arachniotus* and related genera of the Gymnoascaceae. *Persoonia* **6**, 371-380.

Arx, J. A. von (1975). Revision of *Microascus* with the description of a new species. *Persoonia* **8**, 191-197.

Arx, J. A. von (1975). On *Thielavia* and some similar genera of Ascomycetes. *Studies in Mycology* **8**.

Arx, J. A. von (1982). A key to the species of *Gelasinospora*. *Persoonia* **11**, 443-449.

Arx, J. A. von (1986). The ascomycete genus *Gymnoascus*. *Persoonia* **13**, 173-183.

Arx, J. A. von (1987). A re-evaluation of the Eurotiales. *Persoonia* **13**, 273-300. (Keys to families and genera).

Arx, J. A. von, Dreyfuss, M. & Müller, E. (1984). A re-evaluation of *Chaetomium* and the Chaetomiaceae. *Persoonia* **12**, 169-179. (Key to species).

Arx, J. A. von, Figueras, M. J. & Guarro, J. (1988). Sordariaceous Ascomycetes without Ascospore Ejaculation. *Beihefte zur Nova Hedwigia* **94**, 1-104.

Arx, J. A. von, & Gams, W. (1967). Über *Pleurage verruculosa* und die zugehörige *Cladorrhinum-*Konidienform. *Nova Hedwigia* **13**, 198-208.

Arx, J. A. von, Guarro, J. & van der Aa, H. A. (1987). *Asordaria*, a new genus of the Sordariaceae, and a new species of *Melanocarpus*. *Persoonia* **13**, 263-272.

Barrasa, J. M. & Checa, J. (1990). Dothideales del Parque Natural de Monfragüe Cáceres. I. *Boletín Sociedad Micológica de Madrid* **15**, 91-102.

Barrasa, J. M., Lundqvist, N. & Moreno, G. (1986). Notes on the genus *Sordaria* in Spain. *Persoonia* **13**, 83-88.

Bell, A. & Mahoney, D. P. (1995). Coprophilous fungi in New Zealand. I. *Podospora* species with swollen agglutinated perithecial hairs. *Mycologia* **87**, 375-396. (Key and descriptions of 8 spp.).

Bezerra, J. L. & Kimbrough, J. W. (1975). The genus *Lasiobolus* (Pezizales: Ascomycetes). *Canadian Journal of Botany* **53**, 1206-1229. (Key and descriptions of 11 spp.).

Booth, C. (1961). Studies of pyrenomycetes: VI. *Thielavia* with notes on some allied genera. *Mycological Paper* **83**.

Breton, A. & Faurel, L. (1968). Etudes des affinités du genre *Mycorhynchus* Sacc. et description de plusieurs especes nouvelles. *Revue de Mycologie* **32**, 229-258.

Brummelen, J. van (1962). Studies on Discomycetes—II. On four species of *Fimaria*. *Persoonia* **2**, 321-330.

Brummelen, J. van (1962). A World Monograph of the Genera *Ascobolus* and *Saccobolus*. *Persoonia*, Supplement **Volume 1**. (Key and descriptions of 66 spp., and a critical taxonomic treatment).

Brummelen, J. van (1980). Two species of *Ascobolus* new to Britain. *Persoonia* **11**, 87-92.

Brummelen, J. van (1981). The genus *Ascodesmis* (Pezizales, Ascomycetes). *Persoonia* **11**, 333-358.

Brummelen, J. van (1984). Notes on cup-fungi—2. *Lasiobolus*. *Persoonia* **12**, 328-334.

Brummelen, J. van (1986). Notes on cup-fungi—3. On three species of *Cheilymenia*. *Persoonia* **13**, 89-96.

Brummelen, J. van (1990). Notes on cup-fungi—4. On two rare species of *Ascobolus*. *Persoonia* **14**, 203-207.

Cailleux, R. (1971). Recherches sur la mycoflore coprophile centrafricaine. Les genres *Sordaria*, *Gelasinospora*, *Bombardia* (Biologie, Morphologie, Systématique). *Bulletin trimestriel de la Société Mycologique de France* **87**, 461-626 + 27 plates.

Cain, R. F. (1934). Studies of Coprophilous Sphaeriales in Ontario. *University of Toronto Studies, Biological Series*, No. 38. (Reprinted 1968 in Bibliotheca Mycologica, Band 9, by Cramer, Lehre).

Cain, R. F. (1961). Studies of coprophilous Ascomycetes. VII. *Preussia. Canadian Journal of Botany* **39**, 1633-1666.

Cain, R. F. (1962). Studies of coprophilous Ascomycetes. VIII. New species of *Podospora. Canadian Journal of Botany* **40**, 447-490.

Cain, R. F. & Kimbrough, J. W. (1969). *Coprobolus*, a new genus of the tribe Thelebolae (Pezizaceae). *Canadian Journal of Botany* **47**, 1911-1914.

Cain, R. F. & Mirza, J. H. (1972). Three new species of *Arnium. Canadian Journal of Botany* **50**, 333-336.

Cannon, P. F. & Hawksworth, D. L. (1982). A re-evaluation of *Melanospora* Corda and similar Pyrenomycetes, with a revision of the British species. *Botanical Journal of the Linnean Society* **84**, 115-160.

Cannon, P. F., Hawksworth, D. L. & Sherwood-Pike, M. A. (1985). *The British Ascomycotina. An Annotated Checklist.* Commonwealth Agricultural Bureaux, Slough, U. K.

Cano, J. & Guarro, J. (1990). The genus *Aphanoascus. Mycological Research* **94**, 355-377. (Key to species).

Currah, R. S. (1988). An annotated key to the genera of the Onygenales. *Systema Ascomycetum* **7**, 1-12.

Dennis, R. W. G. (1978). *British Ascomycetes.* J. Cramer, Lehre. (or earlier edition, 1968 and 1960 (as *British Cup Fungi and their allies*), The Ray Society, London). (All groups).

Dissing, H. (1987). Three 4-spored *Saccobolus* species from north east Greenland. In *Arctic and Alpine Mycology* II (ed. G. A. Laursen, J. F. Ammirati & S. A. Redhead), pp. 79-86.

Dissing, H. (1989). Four new coprophilous species of *Ascobolus* and *Saccobolus* from Greenland (Pezizales). *Opera Botanica* **100**, 43-50.

Dissing, H. (1992). Notes on the coprophilous pyrenomycete *Sporormia fimetaria*. *Persoonia* **14**, 389-394.

Dissing, H. & Paulsen, M. D. (1976). *Trichophaeopsis tetraspora*, a New Coprophilous Discomycete from Denmark. *Botanisk Tidsskrift* **70**, 147-151.

Elliott, M. E. (1967). *Rutstroemia cuniculi*, a coprophilous species of the Sclerotiniaceae. *Canadian Journal of Botany* **45**, 521-524.

Guarro, J. & Arx, J. A. von (1987). The Ascomycete genus *Sordaria*. *Persoonia* **13**, 301-313. (Key to 14 species and checklist).

Hawksworth, D. L. & Webster, J. (1977). Studies on *Mycorhynchus* in Britain. *Transactions of the British Mycological Society* **68**, 329-340. (Key to 12 spp. and descriptions of some).

Jain, K. & Cain, R. F. (1973). *Mycoarctium*, a new genus in the Thelebolaceae. *Canadian Journal of Botany* **51**, 305-307.

Jeng. R. S., Luck-Allen, E. R. & Cain, R. F. (1977). New species and new records of *Delitschia* from Venezuela. *Canadian Journal of Botany* **55**, 383-392.

Khan. R. S. & Cain, R. F. (1972). Five new species of *Podospora* from East Africa. *Canadian Journal of Botany* **50**, 1649-1661.

Kimbrough, J. W. (1969). North American species of

Thecotheus (Pezizeae, Pezizaceae). *Mycologia* **61**, 99-114. (Key and description of 5 spp.).

Kimbrough, J. W. & Korf. R. P. (1967). A synopsis of the genera and species of the tribe Thelebolae (Pseudoascobolaceae). *American Journal of Botany* **54**, 9-23.

Kimbrough, J. W. & Luck-Allen, E. R. (1974). *Lasiothelebolus*, a new genus of the Thelebolaceae (Pezizales). *Mycologia* **66**, 588-592.

Kimbrough, J. W., Luck-Allen, E. R. & Cain, R. F. (1969). *Iodophanus*, the Pezizeae segregate of Ascophanus (Pezizales). *American Journal of Botany* **56**, 1187-1202. (Key and description of 10 spp.).

Kimbrough, J. W., Luck-Allen, E. R. & Cain, R. F. (1972). North American species of *Coprotus* (Thelebolaceae: Pezizales). *Canadian Journal of Botany* **50**, 957-972. (Key and description of 18 spp.).

Krug, J. C. (1973). An enlarged concept of *Trichobolus* (Thelebolaceae, Pezizales) based on a new eight-spored species. *Canadian Journal of Botany* **51**, 1497-1501. (With key to 4 spp.).

Krug, J. C. (1995). The genus *Fimetariella*. *Canadian Journal of Botany* **73**, 1905-1916. (With key to 8 spp.).

Krug, J. C. & Cain, R. F. (1972). Additions to the genus *Arnium*. *Canadian Journal of Botany* **50**, 367-373. (Key to 25 spp.).

Krug, J. C. & Cain, R. F. (1974). A preliminary treatment of the genus *Podosordaria*. *Canadian Journal of Botany* **52**, 589-605. (Key and descriptions of 10 spp.).

Krug, J. C. & Cain, R. F. (1974). New species of *Hypocopra* (Xylariaceae). *Canadian Journal of Botany* **52**, 809-843. (Descriptions and synoptic key to 30 spp.).

Krug, J. C. & Scott, J. A. (1994). The genus *Bombardioidea*. *Canadian Journal of Botany* **72**, 1302-1310. (Description and key to 4 spp.).

Larsen, K. (1970). The Genus *Saccobolus* in Denmark. *Botanisk Tidsskrift* **65**, 371-389.

Larsen, K. (1971). Danish Endocoprophilous Fungi and Their Sequence of Occurrence. *Botanisk Tidsskrift* **66**, 1-32.

Lohmeyer, T. R. & Benkert, D. (1988). *Poronia erici*—eine neue Art der Xylariales (Ascomycetes). *Zeitschrift fur Mykologie* **54**, 93-102.

Luck-Allen, E. R. & Cain, R. F. (1975). Additions to the genus *Delitschia*. *Canadian Journal of Botany* **53**, 1827-1887. (Key to 46 spp. and descriptions/illustrations of most).

Lundqvist, N. (1967). On spore ornamentation in the Sordariaceae, exemplified by the new cleistocarpous genus *Copromyces*. *Arkiv för Botanik*, Series 2. **6**(7), 327-337.

Lundqvist, N. (1969). *Zygopleurage* and *Zygospermella* (Sordariaceae s. lat., Pyrenomycetes). *Botaniska Notiser* **122**, 353-374.

Lundqvist, N. (1970). New Podosporae (Sordariaceae s. lat., Pyrenomycetes). *Svensk Botanisk Tidskrift* **64**, 409-420.

Lundqvist, N. (1972). Nordic Sordariaceae s. lat. *Symbolae Botanicae Upsalienses* **XX. 1.** 1-314. (Keys and descriptions of *ca* 100 spp., and critical taxonomic discussion).

Lundqvist, N. (1980). On the genus *Pyxidiophora* sensu lato (Pyrenomycetes). *Botaniska Notiser* **133**, 121-144.

Lundqvist, N. (1980). *Wawelia effusa* Lundqvist, spec. nov. (Xylariaceae). *Persoonia* **14**, 417-423.

Malloch, D. & Cain, R. F. (1970). The genus *Arachnomyces*. *Canadian Journal of Botany* **48**, 839-845.

Malloch, D. & Cain, R. F. (1970). Five new genera in the new family of Pseudeurotiaceae. *Canadian Journal of Botany* **48**, 1815-1825.

Malloch, D. & Cain, R. F. (1971). New genera of the Onygenaceae. *Canadian Journal of Botany* **49**, 839-846.

Malloch, D. & Cain, R. F. (1971). Four new genera of cleistothecial Ascomycetes with hyaline ascospores. *Canadian Journal of Botany* **49**, 847-854.

Malloch, D. & Cain, R. F. (1971). New cleistothecial Sordariaceae and a new family, Coniochaetaceae. *Canadian Journal of Botany* **49**, 869-880.

Malloch, D. & Cain, R. F. (1972). New species and combinations of cleistothecial Ascomycetes. *Canadian Journal of Botany* **50**, 61-72.

Minter, D. W. & Webster, J. (1983). *Wawelia octospora* sp. nov., a xerophilous and coprophilous member of the Xylariaceae. *Transactions of the British Mycological Society* **80**, 370-373.

Mirza, J. H. & Cain, R. F. (1969). Revision of the genus *Podospora*. *Canadian Journal of Botany* **47**, 1999-2048.

Moravec, J. (1990). A taxonomic revision of the genus *Cheilymenia*—3. A new generic and infrageneric classification of *Cheilymenia* in a new emendation. *Mycotaxon* **38**, 459-484. (Synopsis of genus, including *Coprobia*).

Moravec, J. (1993). A taxonomic revision of the genus *Cheilymenia*—5. The section *Cheilymenia*. *Czech Mycology* **47**, 7-37.

Moreau, C. (1953) Les Genres *Sordaria* et *Pleurage*. *Encyclopédie mycologique* **25**, 1-330. (*Sordaria* and *Pleurage* (=*Podospora/Schizothecium*), and *Coniochaeta*, *Hypocopra*, *Sporormiella*, *Trichodelitschia*, and other pyrenomycetes for comparison).

Munk, A. (1957). Danish Pyrenomycetes. *Dansk Botanisk Arkiv* **17**(1), 1-491.

Orr, G. F. & Kuehn, H. H. (1971). Notes on Gymnoascaceae. I. A review of eight species. *Mycologia* **63**, 191-203.

Orr, G. F., Kuehn, H. H. & Plunkett, O. A. (1963). A new genus of the Gymnoascaceae with swollen peridial septa. *Canadian Journal of Botany* **41**, 1439-1456. (Key to *Auxarthron* (*Gymnoascus*) species).

Orr, G. F., Kuehn, H. H. & Plunkett, O. A. (1971). The genus *Myxotrichum* Kunze. *Canadian Journal of Botany* **41**, 1457-1480. (Key to species).

Paulsen, M. D. & Dissing, H. (1979). The genus *Ascobolus* in Denmark, *Botanisk Tidsskrift* **74**, 67-78.

Rehm, H. (1887-1895). Ascomyceten: Hysteriaceen und Discomyceten. Vol. 1, Abt. 3 of *Rabenhorst's Kryptogamen-*

Flora. (Discomycetes).

Renny, J. (1874). New species of the genus *Ascobolus*. *Journal of Botany* **12**, 353-357 and 4 plates. (Description and illustration of 6 *Ascozonus* spp.).

Richardson, M. J. (1972). Coprophilous ascomycetes on different dung types. *Transactions of the British Mycological Society* **58**, 37-48.

Samson, R. A. (1972). Notes on *Pseudogymnoascus*, *Gymnoascus* and related genera. *Acta botanica neerlandica* **21**, 517-527.

Seth, H. K. (1970). The genus *Lophotrichus* Benjamin. *Nova Hedwigia* **19**, 591-599.

Valldosera, M. & Guarro, J. (1987). Estudios sobre hongos coprófilos aislados en España. VI. Ascomycetes. *Boletín Sociedad Micológica de Madrid* **12**, 51-56.

Valldosera, M. & Guarro, J. (1988). Some coprophilous ascomycetes from Chile. *Transactions of the British Mycological Society* **90**, 601-605.

Valldosera, M. & Guarro, J. (1989). Estudios sobre hongos coprófilos aislados en España. XI. Ascomycetes. *Boletín Sociedad Micológica de Madrid* **14**, 75-80.

Valldosera, M. & Guarro, J. (1989). Estudios sobre hongos coprófilos aislados en España. XV. El género *Preussia* (*Sporormiella*). *Boletín Sociedad Micológica de Madrid* **14**, 81-94.

Valldosera, M. & Guarro, J. (1992). Estudios sobre

hongos copróphilos en España. XVII. Ascomycotina. *Boletín Sociedad Micológica de Madrid* **17**, 19-37.

Valldosera, M. & Guarro, J. (1992). Estudios sobre hongos copróphilos aislados en España. XVIII. Bibliographic catalogue of Ascomycotina. *Boletín Sociedad Micológica de Madrid* **17**, 39-55.

Valldosera, M., Guarro, J. & Figueras, M. J. (1991). Two interesting coprophilous fungi from Spain. *Mycological Research* **95**, 243-246.

Winter, G. (1884-1887). Ascomyceten: Gymnoasceen und Pyrenomyceten. **Vol. 1,** Abt. 2 of *Rabenhorst's Kryptogamen-Flora.* (Pyrenomycetes).

Yao, Y-J. (1996). Notes on British species of *Lasiobolus. Mycological Research* **100**, 737-739.

Yao, Y-J. & Spooner, B. M. (1996). Notes on British species of *Cheilymenia. Mycological Research* **100**, 361-367.

BASIDIOMYCETE REFERENCES

Moser, M. (1978), in Gams, H. (ed.). *Kleine Kryptogamenflora von Mitteleuropa.* Fischer Verlag.

Moser, M. (1983). *Keys to Agarics and Boleti* (English translation by S. Plant). Roger Phillips, London.

Orton, P. D. & Watling, R. (1979). *British Fungus Flora: Coprinus.* Her Majesty's Stationery Office, Edinburgh.

Phillips, R. (1981). *Mushrooms and other fungi of Great Britain and Europe.* Pan Books, London.

Watling, R. (1982). *British Fungus Flora: Bolbitiaceae.* Her Majesty's Stationery Office, Edinburgh.

PHYCOMYCETE REFERENCES

Benjamin, R. K. (1959). The merosporangiferous Mucorales. *Aliso* **4**, 321-433.

Benjamin, R. K. (1961). Addenda to the merosporangiferous Mucorales. *Aliso* **5**, 11-19.

Benjamin, R. K. (1963). Addenda to the merosporangiferous Mucorales. *Aliso* **5**, 273-288.

Benjamin, R. K. (1965). Addenda to the merosporangiferous Mucorales. *Aliso* **6**, 1-10. (The 4 papers above are an excellent account of *Syncephalis, Piptocephalis, Coemansia* and other unusual allied phycomycetes, republished (1967) as *Bibliotheca Mycologica* **5** by J. Cramer, Lehre).

Gams, W. & Moreau, R. (1959). Le genre *Mortierella*. *Annales scientifiques de l'Université de Besançon*, Series 2 **3**, 95-105.

Hesseltine, C. W. (1955). Genera of Mucorales with a note on their synonymy. *Mycologia* **47**, 344-363. (With good key; many other papers by Hesseltine, with others, in *Mycologia, American Journal of Botany, American Midland Naturalist* and *Lloydia*).

Ingold, C. T. & Zoberi, M. H. (1963). The asexual apparatus of Mucorales in relation to spore liberation. *Transactions of the British Mycological Society* **46**, 115-134.

Naumov, N. A. (1939). Clés des Mucorinées. *Encyclopédie mycologique* **9**, 1-137.

Zycha, H., Siepmann, R. & Linneman, G. (1969). *Mucorales*. J. Cramer, Lehre. (A revision of Zycha, 1935).

GENERAL REFERENCES

Bell, A. (1983). *Dung Fungi: an illustrated guide to coprophilous fungi in New Zealand.* Victoria University Press, Wellington.

Bon, M. (1987). *The Mushrooms and Toadstools of Britain and North-western Europe.* Hodder & Stoughton, London.

Cacialli, G., Caroti, V. & Doveri, F. (1995). *Funghi fimicoli e rari o interssanti del litorale Toscano.* Schede di Micologia **vol. 1.** Fondazione Centro Studi Micologici Dell' A. M. B., Vicenza, Italy.

Domsch, K. H., Gams, W. & Anderson, T. H. (1980). *Compendium of soil fungi.* Academic Press, New York.

Ellis, M. B. & Ellis, J. P. (1988). *Microfungi on Miscellaneous Substrates.* Croom Helm, London & Sydney.

Gilman, J. C. (1957). *A Manual of Soil Fungi.* Iowa State College Press.

Eliasson, U. & Lundqvist, N. (1979). Fimicolous Myxomycetes. *Botaniska Notiser* **132**, 551-568. (A list of 34 spp., with some descriptions and illustrations).

Hawksworth, D. L., Kirk, P. M., Sutton, B. C. & Pegler, D. N. (1995). *Ainsworth & Bisby's Dictionary of the Fungi.* 8th edn. CAB International, Wallingford.

Holden, M. (ed) (1982). Guide to the literature for the identification of British fungi, 4th Edition. *Bulletin of the British Mycological Society* **16**, 36-55; 92-112.

Massee, G., & Salmon, E. S. (1901). Researches on coprophilous fungi. *Annals of Botany, London* **15**, 313-357.

Seifert, K. A., Kendrick, W. B. & Murase, G. (1983). *A key to hyphomycetes on dung*. University of Waterloo Biology Series No. 27.

Webster, J. (1970). Coprophilous Fungi. *Transactions of the British Mycological Society* **54**, 161-180.

Key 1. Ascomycota

1   Ascoma either globose to flask shaped, usually with an easily observable pore or neck (**perithecium** or **pseudothecium**, figs 16, 18, 19, 22, 27, 30, 32, 34-37), or discoid (**apothecium**, figs 1, 3, 4, 7, 11-14). Spores usually 8 in each ascus (less frequently 4, 16, 32, 64, 128 etc.). Asci ellipsoid to cylindrical, borne in a distinct hymenium, thus appearing in fascicles or distinct groups when the fruit body is squashed.   2

-       Ascoma globose to subglobose, lacking a definite pore or neck (**cleistothecium** or **gymnothecium**, figs 38, 39, 46). Asci globose to subglobose, 8-spored, not in a distinct hymenium, appearing quite free when the fruit body is squashed.

                                    Key 2, **148** (p. 45)

2(1)   Ascoma a **perithecium** or **pseudothecium**, usually dark in some part, not opening to a disc but remaining globose or flask shaped. Asci unitunicate, not operculate but often with an apical pore, which may stain blue in iodine, or bitunicate.

Key 2, 1 (p. 24)

- Ascoma an **apothecium**, white or lightly coloured, soft fleshed, opening out to a disc or cushion shape when mature. Asci unitunicate. 3

3(2) Asci opening by an operculum (fig. 8), a bilabiate vertical split down to a subapical ring of thickening (fig. 15), or apparently just bursting. 4

- Asci inoperculate, with an apical pore. 96

4(3) Spores 8 (occasionally 4) in an ascus, colourless, purple or brown. 5

- Spores more than 8 in an ascus, colourless. 77

5(4) Spores remaining colourless. 6

- Spores purple or brown at maturity. 39

6(5) Apothecia with obvious hairs. 7

- Apothecia without obvious hairs (microscopic hairs up to 50μm long may be present). 14

7(6) Hairs brown. Apothecia orange, red orange or yellow orange

(*Cheilymenia*, fig. 1) 8

- Hairs colourless. Apothecia colourless or pinkish.

23

8(7)   Apothecia with stellate hairs. Spores 14-20
       × 8-11µm.

                              Cheilymenia stercorea (figs 1, 2)

-      Apothecia without stellate hairs.   9

9(8)   Spores 14.5-18 × 8-9.5µm. Asci 10-13µm
       diam. Apothecia 2mm diam. or more.

                                          Cheilymenia coprinaria

-      Spores larger, 17 × 10µm or more.   10

10(9) Apothecia reddish orange, up to 1mm
       diam., marginal hairs rooting, wall 2-4µm
       thick. Spores 21-26 × 10-13.8µm.

                                            Cheilymenia fimicola

-      Apothecia pale orange yellow, marginal
       hairs superficial, wall up to 2µm thick.   11

11(10) Asci up to 22µm diam. Spores 17-27 × 10-
       14.5µm.

                                          Cheilymenia pulcherrima

-      Asci wider, 25µm diam. or more. Spores 23-
       26.5 × 13-16.5µm.

                                            Cheilymenia raripila

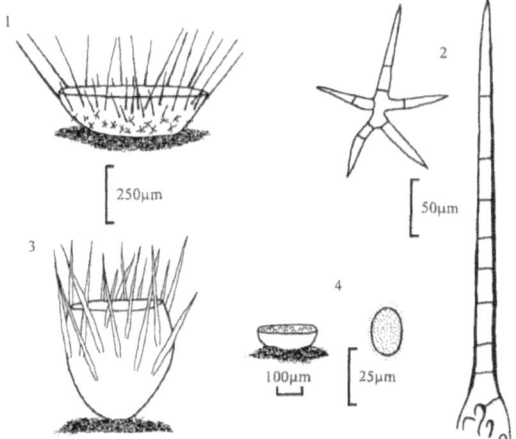

Fig. 1. *Cheilymenia stercorea*, apothecium.
Fig. 2. *C. stercorea*, stellate and rooted hairs.
Fig. 3. *Lasiobolus ciliatus*, apothecium.
Fig. 4. *Iodophanus carneus*, apothecium and spore.

12(7)	Hairs 600µm or longer. Spores 19-23 × 7-10µm.	
		Lasiobolus macrotrichus
-	Hairs shorter, up to 600µm.	13
13(12)	Asci clavate, 20µm diam. or wider. Spores 19-22 × 10.5-13.5µm.	
		Lasiobolus cuniculi
-	Asci cylindrical, up to 20µm diam. Spores 18-22.5 × 9.5-11.5µm.	
		Lasiobolus ciliatus (fig. 3)
14(6)	Asci blue in iodine solution.	15
-	Asci not blue in iodine.	24

25

15(14)   Spores large, 30-42 × 15-18μm, warted, ellipsoid with acute apices.

Thecotheus cinereus

-    Spores smaller, smooth or only finely ornamented   16

16(15)   Apothecia brownish, large, 1cm diam. *(Peziza)* or more.   21

-    Apothecia pale, up to 4mm diam. Asci protruding from hymenium when ripe.   17

17(16)   Apothecia white to pink, up to 2mm diam. Spores finely verruculose, 18-25 × 8-14μm.

Iodophanus carneus (fig. 4)

-    Apothecia pale, variously coloured when fresh, but drying darker. Spores smooth.

(Thecotheus) 18

18(17)   Spores apiculate at each end, smooth.   19

-    Spores not apiculate, 20-22 × 8-10μm.   *Thecotheus agranulosus*

19(18)   Spores with a collar at the base of the apiculus.   20

-    Spores without a collar at the base of the apiculus, 16-21 × 8-12μm.

Thecotheus apiculatus

20(19)   Apothecia white. Spores 20-22 × 10-12μm, apiculus 4-6μm diam.

Thecotheus perplexans

\-   Apothecia yellowish. Spores 12-15 × 7.5-9µm, apiculus 2.5-3.5µm diam.

Thecotheus africanus

21(16)   Spores smooth, without guttules.   22

\-   Spores verruculose or spinulose, 15-18 × 8-9µm, with 1 guttule. Paraphyses with clavate apices, with brown contents. Apothecia asymmetrical, extended on one side.

Peziza pleurota

22(21)   Spores 19-24 × 10.5-14µm. Apothecia yellowish brown, up to 10cm diam.

Peziza vesiculosa

\-   Spores up to 10µm wide.   23

23(22)   Apothecia *ca* 1cm diam., umber with a paler margin. Spores 15-22 × 9-10µm.

Peziza bovina

\-   Apothecia up to 2cm diam., pale brown. Spores 13-16 × 7-9µm.

Peziza fimeti

24(14)   Apothecia robust, up to 4mm diam., orange or with brownish or purple tints.   25

\-   Apothecia smaller, rarely more than 1mm, pale, yellowish green, orange, grey or chestnut.   32

25(24)   Apothecia orange or red.   26

27

-       Apothecia discrete, brownish or   (*Fimaria*)
        purple.   27

26(25) Apothecia crowded, 1-3mm diam., orange,
        with a granular surface. Asci up to 190 ×
        15µm. Spores 15-18.5 × 7-9.5µm.
        Paraphyses strongly clavate to apex up to
        14µm diam, filled with orange granules.
                                    Coprobia granulata

-       Apothecia discrete, 1-2mm diam., orange or
        red. Asci 240 × 10-12µm. Spores 12-15 × 7-
        8µm. Paraphyses yellow, only slightly
        swollen from 2µm to 3-4µm at apex.
                                Ascophanus bresadolae

27(25) Spores 8-9.5 × 4-4.5µm.   *Fimaria equina*

-       Spores larger.   28

28(27) Spores 20-38 × 10-13µm.   *Fimaria hepatica*

-       Spores shorter.   29

29(28) Spores 10-13 × 7-9µm.   *Fimaria porcina*

-       Spores 13-17 × 7-11µm.   30

30(29) Disc punctate with asci. Paraphysis tips
        swollen up to 3-5µm. Spores 14.5-16 × 9.5-
        11µm.
                                    Fimaria leporum

-       Disc not punctate with asci. Paraphysis
        tips not or only slightly swollen.   31

31(30) Apothecia pale yellowish. Spores 13-15.5 ×
        7.5-8.5µm.

                                Fimaria theioleuca

-       Apothecia chestnut/purplish brown.
        Spores 14-17 × 7-8.5µm.

                                Fimaria cervaria

32(24) Spores less than 10µm long.   33

-       Spores mostly longer than 10µm.   36

33(32) Paraphyses markedly capitate to 5-6µm,
        with yellowish green contents. Apothecia
        dull at first, yellowish at maturity. Spores
        7-10 × 2-4.5µm.

                        Thelebolus microsporus (fig. 5)

-       Paraphyses only slightly inflated above,
        without coloured contents. Apothecia
        whitish or grey.   34

34(33) Spores 5-7 × 3-4µm. Asci 38-42 × 6-7µm.
        Apothecia smoky grey, 0.3-0.4mm diam.

                                Ascophanus cinerellus

-       Spores larger. Apothecia pale, white or
        yellowish.   35

35(34) Apothecia up to 1.2mm diam. Asci short
        stalked, 40-55 × 8-12µm. Spores 7.5-9 × 4.5-
        5.5µm.

                                Coprotus glaucellus

-       Apothecia 0.2-0.5mm diam. Asci attenuate

below, 65-85 × 10-15μm. Spores 8-10 × 5-6.5μm.

Coprotus lacteus

36(32) Apothecia chestnut brown up to 1mm diam. Asci 160 × 13μm. Spores 13-16 x 8-11μm. Paraphyses forked, with swollen tips.

Ascophanus misturae

- Apothecia lighter coloured. Asci less than 150μm long. 37

37(36) Spores 14-18 × 9-11μm. Apothecia pale yellow/orange, up to 1.5mm diam. Asci cylindrical, 110-150 × 12-15μm. Paraphyses yellowish, slightly inflated to 4-5μm at apices.

Coprotus ochraceus

- Spores less than 15μm long. Apothecia up to 0.6mm diam. Asci less than 100μm long. 38

Fig. 5. *Thelebolus microsporus*, ascus and paraphysis.
Fig. 6. *Ascodesmis microscopica*, ascospores.

38(37)   Apothecia bright yellow. Asci cylindrical
         clavate, attenuate below, 65-90 × 10-15μm.
         Spores 12-14 × 6-8.5μm. Paraphyses
         branched, apices inflated to 4-5μm, with
         yellow contents.

Coprotus aurorus

-        Apothecia white/pale yellow, with darker
         margin. Asci broadly clavate, stalked below
         40-55 × 15-30μm. Spores 9-15 × 6.5-9.5μm.
         Paraphyses inflated above to 5-8μm,
         hyaline.

Coprotus granuliformis

39(5)   Spores spherical or broadly ellipsoid,
         brown, ornamented with warts,
         anastomosing ridges or a reticulum. Asci
         clavate. Apothecium without excipulum.

(*Ascodesmis*, fig. 6) 40

-        Spores ellipsoid or spherical, hyaline at
         first, then purple, becoming brown at
         maturity; epispore smooth, finely
         verruculose, warted or cracked. Asci
         cylindrical. Excipulum present.   45

31

| 40(39) | Spores 18-21.5 × 13.5-17.5µm. | *Ascodesmis macrospora* |
| - | Spores up to 16µm. | 41 |

| 41(40) | Spores ± spherical, L/B ratio mostly up to 1.2. | 42 |
| - | Spores ± broadly ellipsoidal, L/B ratio mostly 1.2 or more. | 43 |

42(41) Spores ornamented with round warts, 8.5-11 × 8.3-10µm.

Ascodesmis nana

- Spores ornamented with a network of ridges, 10.5-14 × 9-12µm.

Ascodesmis sphaerospora

43(41) Spores with a prominent reticulum of ridges (fig. 6), 11-15.5 × 8-13.5µm. Apothecia 150-300µm diam.

Ascodesmis microscopica (fig. 6)

- Spore ornament not a reticulum. 44

44(43) Spores with 1 simple or branched ridge and isolated or occasionally connected warts, 11-14.5 × 7-11.5µm. Apothecia up to 500µm diam.

Ascodesmis porcina

- Spores with isolated warts, some joined to form short ridges, but not a reticulum, often capitate, 9.5-12.5 × 7.5-10µm.

Apothecia 50-150μm diam.

> *Ascodesmis nigricans*

45(39) Spores separate in the ascus.   (*Ascobolus*) 46

- Spores firmly joined together, both in the ascus and after ejection (fig. 10).

> (*Saccabolus*) 66

46(45) Spores spherical.   47

- Spores ellipsoid.   48

47(46) Spores 10.5-13.5μm, epispore with numerous but isolated warts.

> *Ascobolus brassicae* (figs 8, 9)

- Spores 11.5-13.5(15)μm, epispore with subparallel occasionally anastomosing lines.

> *Ascobolus crosslandii*

48(46) Spores very large, mostly 50-70 × 25-35μm, almost oblong with rounded ends, typically with few cracks in the epispore.

> *Ascobolus immersus* (figs 7, 9)

- Spores smaller, with epispore smooth, warted or with cracks.   49

49(48) Epispore strongly and irregularly wrinkled with a vesiculose layer of pigment, 11.6-16 × 6.5-9.3μm. Paraphyses capitate up to 18μm. Apothecia up to 0.6mm diam.

> *Ascobolus rhytidiosporus*

-       Epispore not strongly wrinkled/vesiculose.   50

50(49) Epispore basically smooth or warted,
        perhaps with a few irregular cracks.   51

-       Epispore with a clear pattern of cracks or
        lines.   56

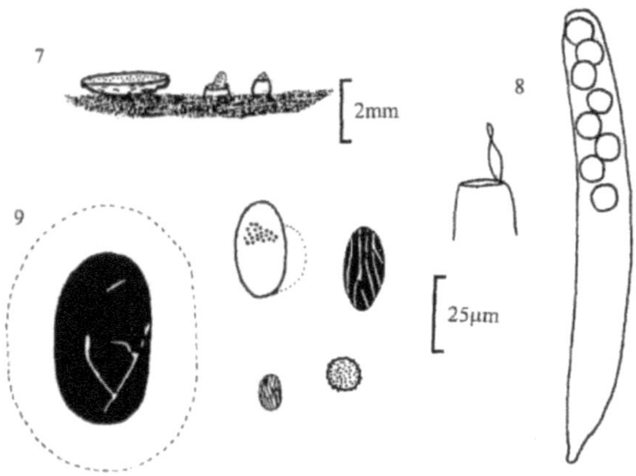

Fig. 7. Apothecia of, from left, *Ascobolus furfuraceus, A. immersus* and *A. albidus.*
Fig. 8. *A. brassicae,* ascus with spores and detail of operculum.
Fig. 9. Ascospores of, clockwise from left, *A. immersus, A. stictoideus, A. albidus, A. brassicae* and *A. crenulatus.*

51(50) Spores up to 25μm long.   52
-       Spores longer, 25μm or more.   54

52(51) Epispore smooth, finely granular or
        punctate. Gelatinous material unilateral,
        not surrounding spore.   53

-       Epispore warted, spores 18.5-21(22.5) ×
        (9)10-11.5μm, surrounded by gelatinous
        sheath.

34

53(52)   Spores 18-24 × 10-13μm. Hymenial mucus greenish yellow. Excipulum not brown.
                              Ascobolus mancus

-        Spores 20-25 × 11-13μm. Hymenial mucus sulphur yellow. Excipulum with rich brown intercellular pigment.
                              Ascobolus boudieri

54(51)   Epispore smooth or finely granular, spores 23-29(32) × 12-17μm.
                              Ascobolus elegans

-        Epispore warted.   55

55(54)   Spores with a regular pattern of warts and intact epispore, 26-32 × 15-17.5μm.
                              Ascobolus stictoideus (fig. 9)

-        Spores with irregular patches of thicker pigment, especially at the poles, 28-35 × 16-18μm.
                              Ascobolus degluptus

56(50)   Spores mostly 18 × 10μm or larger.   57
-        Spores mostly smaller than 20 × 10μm.   61

57(56)   Apothecia small, mostly up to 1mm diam., colourless. Spores 20-35 × 11-14μm, epispore cracks distant, irregular, often anastomosing.
                              Ascobolus albidus (figs 7, 9)

-        Apothecia larger, usually 1mm diam. or
         more, disc yellowish, greenish, purplish or
         brownish.   58

58(57)   Apothecia crowded, purplish or purplish
         brown with intercellular pigment. Spores
         18-28 × 10-12µm, with longitudinal
         anastomosing cracks.

                                  Ascobolus roseopurpurascens

-        Apothecia yellowish or greenish.   59

59(58)   Spores 17-22 × 9.5-12µm with a few widely
         spaced and irregularly oriented cracks.

                                          Ascobolus michaudii

-        Spores with closely spaced, ± longitudinal,
         cracks, with varying degrees of
         anastomosis.   60

60(59)   Apothecia furfuraceous, sessile. Ascus wall
         blue in iodine. Spores 19-28 × 10-14µm.

                                  Ascobolus furfuraceus (fig. 7)

-        Apothecia smooth, substipitate. Ascus wall
         only faintly blue in iodine. Spores 19-22 ×
         9.5-13µm.

                                          Ascobolus perplexans

61(56)   Apothecia large, stipitate, 5-10mm diam.
         Spores 16-19.5 × 8.5-10µm, with
         subparallel, longitudinal, only rarely
         anastomosing lines.

                                           Ascobolus lignatilis

-        Apothecia up to 2mm diam.   62

62(61)   Apothecia white.   63

-        Apothecia yellow, green or brownish.   64

63(62)   Spores 13-17 × 7.5-8.5μm, with a coarse
         reticulum of fine cracks when mature. Only
         recorded on grouse, capercaillie etc.
         (Tetraonidae) dung.
                               Ascobolus carletonii

-        Spores 16-20 × 8-10μm, with a pattern of
         longitudinal anastomosing cracks. Only
         recorded on deer dung.
                            Ascobolus sacchariferus

64(62)   Spores 14.5-16 × 8-9μm, epispore lines not
         densely crowded.
                                 Ascobolus cervinus

-        Spores smaller, epispore with densely
         crowded, rarely anastomosing cracks.   65

65(64)   Apothecia greenish yellow, furfuraceous,
         with crenulate margin. Spores 9.5-15 × 6-
         8μm.
                          Ascobolus crenulatus (fig. 9)

-        Apothecia brownish yellow to brown,
         smooth, with undifferentiated margin.
         Spores 12.5-14.5 × 7-8.5μm.
                                 Ascobolus minutus

66(45)   Asci 4-spored. Spore clusters 42-58 × 14-

20μm. Spores 16.5-23 × 9.5-12μm, smooth
to finely punctate, but with a thick cap or
girdle of reticulated or warted pigment.

Saccobolus quadrisporus

\-   Asci 8-spored.   67

67(66) Spore clusters ± globular, 17-26(39) × 15-
20μm.   68

\-   Spore clusters elongated, 2-3 times as long
as wide.   69

68(67) Spore clusters compact, subglobose, with
only the exposed surface of spores
pigmented, ornamented with small and
coarse warts.

Saccobolus dilutellus

\-   Spores loosely united in cluster,
ornamented with small isolated warts
covering most of their surface.

Saccobolus globuliferellus

69(67) Apothecia yellow. Spores in 4 rows of 2
longitudinally arranged spores (fig. 10).   70

\-   Apothecia hyaline or violaceous (some
mature darker). Spores in 2 rows of 3 and 1
row of 2 (fig. 10).   73

70(69) Spore clusters 40μm or longer.   71
\-   Spore clusters up to 40μm long.   72

71(70) Spore clusters 50-71 × 16-25μm. Spores 22-

29 × 8.5-14.5µm, smooth or rarely finely
punctate, with distant irregular cracks.
Saccobolus glaber (fig. 10)

\-   Spore clusters 43-51 × 14-17µm. Spores 16-
22 × 7.5-9µm, with fine isolated warts.
Saccobolus citrinus

72(70)   Spores 14-17.5(19.5) × 7.5-8.5(10)µm, easily
separated at maturity. Spore clusters
becoming shorter and more rounded with
maturity. Apothecia up to 300µm diam.,
inconspicuous due to their solitary nature
and the predominantly brownish colour
due to the mature spores.
Saccobolus truncatus (fig. 10)

\-   Spores 11.5-13.5 × 5.5-6.5µm.   *Saccobolus minimus*

73(69)   Apothecia white, covered with tapering
squamules composed of septate hyphae.
Spore clusters 38-43 × 15-17µm. Spores 16-
17.5 × 7-8.5µm, smooth or finely punctate.
Saccobolus caesariatus

\-   Apothecia not white, without tapering
scales.   74

74(73)   Spore clusters mostly over 40µm long.   75

\-   Spore clusters mostly under 40µm long.   76

75(74)   Spore clusters 38-62 × 14-19µm. Spores 13-
21.5 × 6.5-9.5µm, smooth, finely warted or
with reticulate cracks. Apothecia 0.2-2mm

diam.

Saccobolus versicolor (fig. 10)

- Spore clusters 42-60 × 18-24µm. Spores very coarsely warted, 17.5-23 × 8.5-10µm (inc. warts).

Saccobolus beckii

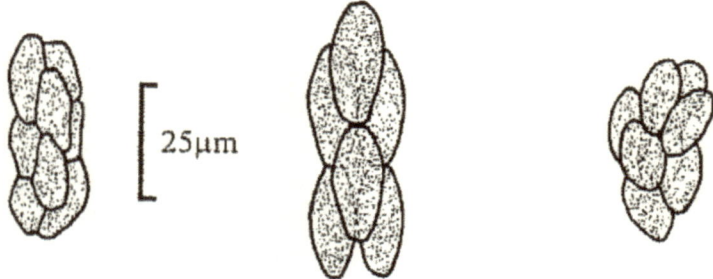

Fig. 10. Spore clusters of, from left, *Saccobolus versicolor, S. glaber* and *S. truncatus*

76(74) Spore clusters compact, 26-43 × 13-19µm. Spores 13.5-18 × 7.5-9.5µm, epispore with fine or coarse warts. Apothecia 0.3-0.8mm diam.

Saccobolus obscurus

- Spore clusters elongated, 28-37 × 10-13µm. Spores 10-14.5 × 5-7.5µm, epispore smooth or very finely granular. Apothecia 0.1-0.3mm diam.

Saccobolus depauperatus

77(4) Asci operculate or bursting, without a subapical ring. Spores ellipsoid.   78

- Apothecia white, often minutely hairy at the margin. Ascus dehiscing by a vertical

slit; the slit is prevented from running
right down the ascus by a subapical ring of
thickening. Spores ellipsoid-fusiform.

(*Ascozonus*, figs 14, 15) 90

78(77) Asci 16-spored. Spores ellipsoid, 11-16 × 7-
10µm.

Coprotus sexdecemsporus

- Asci more than 16-spored. 79

79(78) Asci 32-spored. 80

- Asci more than 32-spored. 84

80(79) Asci very large, nearly 0.5mm long, spores
30-35 × 13-17µm (32-40 × 20-24µm in
Kimbrough, 1969). Apothecia pale
coloured.

Thecotheus pelletieri

- Asci and spores smaller. 81

81(80) Spores 10µm or longer. 83

- Spores up to 10µm long. 82

82(81) Spores ellipsoid, with minute scattered
warts visible under oil-immersion, 7-9 × 4-
4.5µm. Apothecia densely crowded, 90-
120µm diam., with 8-13 asci. Asci 32-55 ×
16-18µm with (24-)32 spores. Paraphyses
1.5-2µm, clavate to 4-4.5µm.

Thelebolus caninus

41

-   Spores subacute at apices, *ca* 6 × 4µm
    (described as 'minute'; this value is
    suggested by Boudier's comparison with *R.
    dubius*, for which measurements are given).
    Apothecia densely crowded, tawny
    yellowish-brown.

    Ryparobius brunneus

83(81) Spores 10-12.5 × 5-7.5µm. Asci clavate, 75-
    100 × 20-30µm. Paraphyses enlarged to 6µm
    at apex.

    Coprotus albidus

-   Spores 13.5-17.5 × 7-8µm. Asci 10-15 per
    apothecium, 120-175 × 50-75µm.
    Paraphyses filiform.

    Coprotus rhyparobioides

84(79) Asci with up to 64 spores.   85

-   Asci with many more than 64 spores—
    impractical to count.   86

85(84) Asci 64-spored, broad clavate with short
    stalk, 80-130 × 30-60µm. Spores 8-12 × 4-
    7µm.

    Coprotus niveus

-   Asci broadly clavate with up to 64 spores,
    60-100 × 20-30µm. Spores 7-10 × 4.5-5.5µm.
    Apothecia superficial, on the surface of the
    substrate, yellowish brown, gregarious,
    united into a crust.

    Thelebolus crustaceus

42

86(84) Apothecia superficial, 400-600µm diam.,
with prominent, acuminate, superficial, 1-
2-septate hairs, 80-190µm long, often
roughened towards their apex, with one
1000+-spored ascus, 110-240 × 15-27µm.
Spores very variable, 6.5-16 × 3.7-8.8µm
(mostly 7.5-13 × 4.5-7µm).

Lasiobolus monascus

- Apothecia minute, rarely above 350µm
diam., globose and immersed in substrate
when young. Asci broad globose, with
100-200 spores. Usually only 1-3 asci in
each apothecium, which dehisce by
bursting at the apex.   87
(Other *Ryparobius* spp. will key out here
[e.g. *R. dubius*, *R. myriosporus*, *R. pachyascus*
and *R. polysporus*]. They all have scattered
to gregarious, immersed to semi-immersed
apothecia 100-200µm diam., with relatively
few asci, each with 100-250 ellipsoid to
subacuminate *ca* 5-7 × 3-4µm spores. There
are insufficient modern observations to
allow their identification and separation
with confidence).

87(86) Apothecia with a few, but obvious, setae.
Spores 9 × 7µm or larger.   88

- Apothecia without setae. Spores ellipsoid,
6-9 × 3.5-4µm.   89

88(87) Spores ellipsoid, 9-11 × 7-9µm. Setae up to
600µm long.

Trichobolus zukalii

-        Spores subglobose, 11-12 × 10-11µm. Setae
         up to 300µm long.

                              Trichobolus sphaerosporus (fig. 11)

89(87)   Apothecia and asci large, 170-250µm diam.

                                 Thelebolus stercoreus (fig. 12)

-        Apothecia and asci small, rarely above 80-
         90µm diam.

                                    Thelebolus nanus (fig. 13)

90(77)   Asci 16(-24)-spored. Spores not closely
         aggregated into an imbricated mass, 13-14 ×
         6µm (8-9 × 4µm)[1]. Apothecial hairs
         rough, subulate.

                                   Ascozonus parvisporus

-        Asci with 32 or more spores.   91

91(90)   Asci 32-spored. Spores 16.5-18 × 4.5-5µm
         (11-12 × 3-3.5µm)[1]. Apothecia with a
         single row of sharp, pointed, roughened
         hairs.

                                     Ascozonus crouanii

-        Asci more than 32-spored.   92

92(91)   Asci 48-spored. Spores spindle-shaped, 12-
         14.5 × 2.5-4µm.

                                      Ascozonus leveillei

-        Asci more than 48-spored.   93

93(92)   Asci 64-spored.   94

94(93)   Apothecia with a short base of globose
         cells, with minutely roughened marginal
         hairs up to 30 × 8µm. Spores elliptic-fusoid,
         12-14 × 3-5µm.

                    Ascozonus woolhopensis (figs 14, 15)

-        Apothecia sessile, with aseptate smooth
         hairs. Spores 21 × 7.5µm (13-14 × 4.5-5µm)
         [1].

                              Ascozonus cunicularis

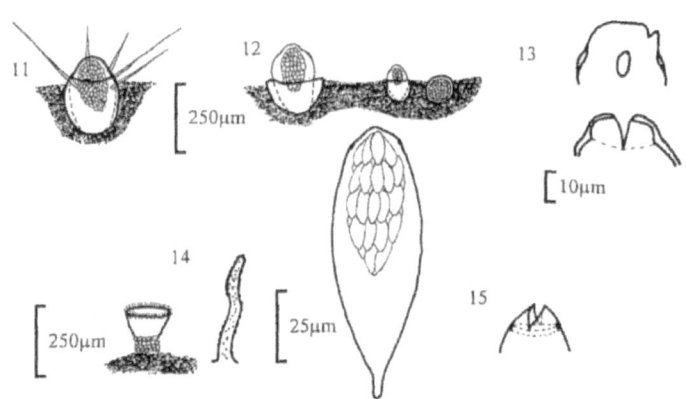

Fig. 11. *Trichobolus sphaerosporus*, apothecium.
Fig. 12. *Thelebolus stercoreus*, apothecium.
Fig. 13. *T. nanus*, mature and immature apothecia, and detail of ascus
dehiscence.
Fig. 14. *Ascozonus woolhopensis*, apothecium and apothecial hair.
Fig. 15. *A. woolhopensis*, ascus with spores and detail of dehiscence.

95(93)   Apothecia with a short base of globose
         cells, with short, irregular hairs. Asci 64-
         96-spored Spores elliptic-fusoid, 14-14.5 ×
         5-5.5µm (10-15 × 3.5-4µm)[1].

                              Ascozonus leveillanus

45

-          Apothecia sessile, dotted with hairs in
           connate groups of 2-3. Asci with 128 or
           more spores. Spores 10 × 5µm (7 × 3.5µm)
           [1].

                                        Ascozonus subhirtus

96(3)   Apothecia stalked.   97

-          Apothecia not stalked.   98

97(96)   Apothecia up to 2mm diam., with a short
           cylindrical stalk, light brown. Asci 150 ×
           10µm. Spores hyaline, with 2 oil drops,
           occasionally 1-septate, 13-15 × 4.5µm.
                                          Lanzia cuniculi

-          Apothecia up to 3mm diam., pale
           olivaceous to grey, with a long, slender,
           reddish-brown stalk arising from a
           sclerotium in the dung. Asci 30-40 × 4-
           5µm. Spores ellipsoid, grey-brown, 4-4.5 ×
           2µm.
                                   Martininia panamaensis

98(96)   Spores 7-11(14) × 1.75-2.75µm. ellipsoid,
           ellipsoid-fusiform or slightly clavate.
           Apothecia yellowish brown when fresh,
           drying darker, up to 1mm diam. Asci 42-
           60 × 7.5-9µm, pore weakly blue in iodine.
                                         Pezizella albula

-          Spores and asci smaller.   99

99(98)   Spores linear, 3-5 × 1µm. Asci 30 × 5µm,

                              46

cylindrical with a short stipe. Paraphyses not clavate but fused to form an epithecium. Apothecia pale pellucid, 0.5-1mm diam.

Orbilia leporina

- Spores longer, subulate, curved. 100

100(99) Spores 7-8.5 × 1.2-1.8µm. Asci 36-40 × 3-5µm, gradually tapering to a short base. Paraphyses enlarged to 3µm at apex, covered with brown granules. Apothecia light brown, 0.4-1.mm diam.

Orbilia fimicola

- Spores 8-10.55 × 0.9-1µm. Asci 30-45 × 3µm, cylindrical-clavate with narrow tapering base and truncate apex. Paraphyses 2µm diam., the tips with a crust-like secretion fusing together to form a shiny epithecium. Apothecia white to yellowish, 180-700µm diam.

Orbilia fimicoloides

Key 2. Perithecial, pseudothecial, cleistothecial and gymnothecial fungi

1 (key 1,2)	Perithecia occurring singly or in groups, but directly on the dung or buried in it (figs 16, 28, 19, 22, 27, 30, 32, 34-36).	2
-	Perithecia occurring in or on a mass of fungal tissue (stroma) growing in or on the dung (figs 32, 37).	135
2(1)	Spores black, brown or dark olive-greenish.	3
-	Spores hyaline or pale coloured, at least under the microscope (may be coppery red *en masse*).	117
3(2)	Spores smooth, without an ornamentation of hyaline pits.	4
-	Spores 1-celled, ornamented with hyaline pits.	
	(*Gelasinospora*)	114
4(3)	Perithecia dark, olive, brown or black.	5
-	Perithecia reddish brown, orange or golden, globose, with a neck. Spores black, limoniform.	116
5(4)	Perithecia globose, surmounted by a dense tuft of greyish green hairs, which may be branched or simple, straight or curly. Spores olivaceous, limoniform. Asci clavate, soon	

disappearing. (A large genus not characteristic of dung, but occurring occasionally).

Chaetomium (fig. 16)

\-   Perithecia more pyriform, or if globose then with a distinct neck, may be setose but not densely hairy, with clavate or cylindrical asci.   6

6(5)   Each spore composed of 4 or more cells in a row (figs 17, 21). Asci bitunicate (figs 20, 23).   7

\-   Spores 1- or 2-celled. Asci bitunicate or unitunicate.   29

7(6)   Spores 16-32-celled, united firmly together in a bundle both in the ascus and after discharge. Germ slits usually absent.

(*Sporormia*) 8

\-   Spores each with 4 or more cells, each spore free and surrounded by its own gelatinous sheath. Germ slits usually present.

(*Sporormiella*) 11

8(7)   Spores 16-20-celled.   9
\-   Spores 29-32-celled, 130-160 × 4-6μm.   *Sporormia mirabilis*

9(8)   Spores 16-celled, 85-116 × 5-6.5μm.   *Sporormia fimicola*

\-   Spores smaller.   10

10(9)   Spores 16-celled, 37-45 × 3μm. Asci 50-60 × 10-12μm.

Sporormia sp. (fig. 17)

[recorded as *S. fimetaria* by Richardson (1972); see also Bell (1983) and Dissing (1992)]

- Spores 16-20-celled, 50-57 × 3.5-4.5μm. Asci 70-80 × 12-16μm.

Sporormia fimetaria

(These two taxa may represent the extremes of *S. fimetaria*).

11(7)	Spores 4-celled.	12
-	Spores more than 4-celled.	22

12(11)	Spores more than 65-70μm long.	13
-	Spores less than 65-70μm long.	15

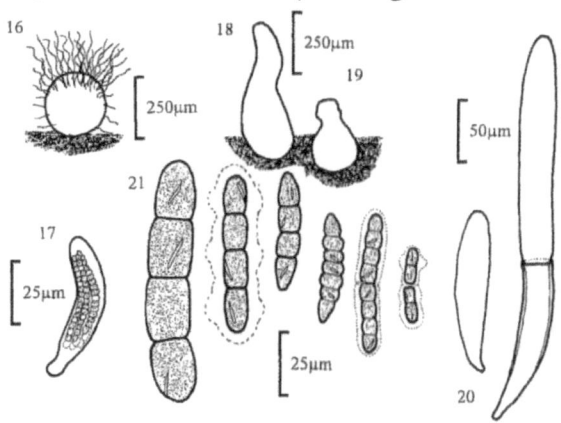

Fig. 16. *Chaetomium* sp., perithecium and spore.
Fig. 17. *Sporormia* sp., ascus and spores.
Fig. 18. *Sporormiella ovina*, pseudothecium.
Fig. 19. *S. intermedia*, pseudothecium.
Fig. 20. *S. intermedia*, immature bitunicate ascus and mature ascus with outer layer ruptured.
Fig. 21. Ascospores of, from left, *S. ovina*, *S. intermedia* (with

50

gelatinous sheath characteristic of the genus), *S. lageniformis*, *S. vexans*, *S. bipartis* and *S. minima*.

13(12)	Spores 65-95 × 15-18μm.	*Sporormiella megalospora*
-	Spores longer than 90μm.	14

14(13)   Spores 90-118 × 15-20μm. Asci tapering gradually from the broadest part near the apex to a 'stipe'.

Sporormiella ovina (figs 18, 21)

-   Spores 91-114 × (14)18-21μm. Asci cylindrical, abruptly contracted below to a short 'stipe'.

Sporormiella borealis

15(12)	Spores mostly less than 35μm long.	16
-	Spores mostly between 35-60μm long.	19

16(15)	Spores less than 25μm long.	17
-	Spores 25-35(38)μm long.	18

17(16)   Spores (15)17-24(26) × 5-7μm, end cells broadly conical. Ascospores uniseriate. Asci 120-135μm long. Pseudothecia 250-300μm diam.

Sporormiella pulchella

-   Spores 16-22 × 4.5-5.5μm, end cells subovate. Ascospores biseriate. Asci 95-125μm long. Pseudothecia 300-350μm diam.

18(16)   Spores 30-38.5 × 5.5-6.5μm. Asci clavate,
         tapering gradually below to a 'stipe'.
                                          Sporormiella leporina

-        Spores 27-36(38) × 4-6(8)μm, tending to
         break in two at the middle septum. Asci
         cylindrical, abruptly contracted below.
                                 Sporormiella minima (fig. 21)

19(15)   Spores with end cells rounded. Asci
         cylindrical, abruptly contracted below.   20

-        Spores with end cells tapered and slightly
         conical. Asci clavate, tapering gradually to
         a long stalk.   21

20(19)   Spores 45-65 × 8-11.5μm.
                            Sporormiella intermedia (figs 19-21)

-        Spores 38-46 × 6.5-8μm.   *Sporormiella australis*

21(19)   Spores 45-60 × 11.5-14μm, germ slits
         parallel with long axis.
                                      Sporormiella grandispora

-        Spores 35-45(48) × 7-9(10)μm.
                              Sporormiella lageniformis (fig. 21)

         Spores 5-celled, 70-80 × 17-   *Sporormiella*
22(11)   19μm.   *pentamera*

-        Spores more than 5-celled.   23

23(22)   Spores 7- or 8-celled.   24

| - | Spores 13-celled, 46-60 × 9-10μm. | *Sporormiella antarctica* |

| 24(23) | Spores 7-celled. | 25 |
| - | Spores 8-celled. | 26 |

25(24) Spores 40-55 × 7-9μm, readily disarticulating, the end cells longer than wide, the rest shorter than wide.
Sporormiella vexans (fig. 21)

- Spores 70-80 × 16-18μm, end cells rounded.
Sporormiella heptamera

| 26(24) | Spores mostly longer than 45μm. | 27 |
| - | Spores less than 50μm long, not disarticulating at the central septum. | 28 |

27(26) Spores 45-60 × 5-7.5μm, disarticulating at the central septum, all cells the same width.
Sporormiella bipartis (fig. 21)

- Spores 50-59 × 10-12μm, not disarticulating, 3rd cell down wider than the others.
Sporormiella corynespora

28(26) Spores (33)37-40(49) × 7-9μm, cylindrical. Asci abruptly contracted below.
Sporormiella pascua

- Spores 40-48 × 7-8μm, fusiform cylindrical. Asci gradually tapered below.

29(6)   Spores obviously 2-celled at maturity.   30

\-   Spores 1-celled, or appearing 1-celled at maturity. (Those of *Podospora, Schizothecium* etc. are 2-celled in early stages of their development, but only one cell matures to become pigmented; the other remains hyaline, often collapses, and may be difficult to see).   47

30(29)   Spores 23-28 × 13-17μm, upper cell dark, 15-19μm, with close, blunt spines giving the impression of a pitted spore surface, with apical germ pore, the lower cell hyaline, 6-8.5μm, smoky-brown. Asci unitunicate, 4-spored. Perithecia 400μm diam.

Apiosordaria verruculosa (fig. 24)

\-   Both cells of spore similar in shape, size and colour.   31

31(30)   Asci unitunicate. Spores with a 'gelatinous' appendage at each end. Perithecial neck with setae.   32

\-   Asci bitunicate. Spores without gelatinous appendages, although a sheath may be present.   33

32(31)   Spores 38-48 × 11-14μm, appendages longitudinally fibrillate.

Zygospermella striata

54

-       Spores 46-68 × 11-17μm, appendages
hollow, not fibrillate.
                                  Zygospermella insignis (fig. 25)

33(31) Spores with each end truncated by a germ
        pore. Pseudothecia with dark bristles at
        neck.
                                  (*Trichodelitschia*) 34

-       Spores with rounded ends and germ slits
        along the sides. Pseudothecial neck smooth
        or hairy, but without setae.
                                  (*Delitschia*, fig. 26) 36

34(33) Spores 28-34 × 9-12μm.   *Trichodelitschia aedelphica*
-       Spores smaller.   35

35(34) Spores 20-27.5 × 8-11μm.
                        Trichodelitschia bisporula (figs 22, 23)
-       Spores 18-21 × 6-7μm.   *Trichodelitschia munkii*

36(33) Asci *ca* 256-spored. Spores 14-15 × 6-8μm.
                                  Delitschia myriaspora

-       Asci 8-spored.   37

37(36) Spores less than 20μm long.   38
-       Spores more than 20μm long.   41

38(37) Spores 8-11 × 3-5μm.   *Delitschia perpusilla*
-       Spores 10-20μm long.   39

39(38)   Spores 10-14 × 5-6µm.   *Delitschia marchalii*

-       Spores longer.   40

40(39)   Spores 14-18 × 6-10µm, uniseriate. Asci 70-
90 × 7-16µm.

                                   Delitschia niesslii

-       Spores (16)18-20(22.5) × 6-7.5µm, biseriate.
Asci 80-145 × 20-25µm.

                      Delitschia consociata (fig. 26)

41(37)   Spores mostly wider than 20µm.   42

-       Spores mostly less than 20µm wide.   43

42(41)   Spores 50-64 × 19-23µm.   *Delitschia furfuracea*

-       Spores 50-70 × 25-33µm.

                      Delitschia winteri (fig. 26)

43(41)   Spores 20-25 × 4.5-6µm, the cells slightly
tapered and almost completely separated.
Pseudothecia hairless, globose, *ca* 200µm
diam.

                      Delitschia leptospora (fig. 26)

-       Spores longer and wider.   44

44(43)   Spores transversely septate.   45

-       Spores obliquely septate, deeply constricted
at the septum, 35-50 × 15-18µm.

                      Delitschia didyma

45(44) Pseudothecia hairy. Spores 37-50 × 17-20μm, not deeply constricted at the septum.

Delitschia chaetomioides

- Pseudothecia smooth. 46

46(45) Spores biseriate, 45-55 × 13-16μm, one cell usually larger than the other, deeply constricted at the septum and readily separating.

Delitschia canina

- Spores uniseriate, 40-55 × 16-21μm, both cells equal.

Delitschia patagonica

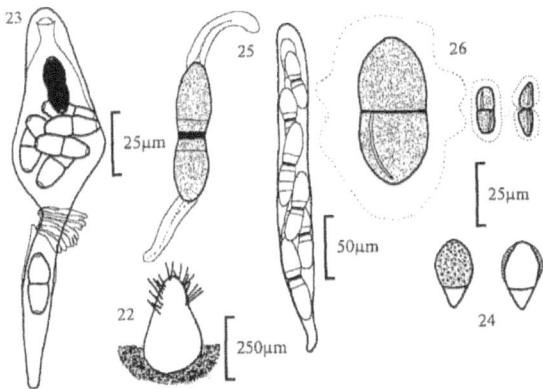

Fig. 22. *Trichodelitschia bisporula*, pseudothecium.
Fig. 23. *T. bisporula*, expanded ascus broken through the outer wall, with spores.
Fig. 24. *Apiosordaria verruculosa*, ascospores.
Fig. 25. *Zygospermella insignis*, ascus and ascospore.
Fig. 26. Ascospores of, from left, *Delitschia winteri*, *D. consociata* and *D. leptospora*.

47(29) Spores with colourless 'gelatinous'

secondary appendages (caudae, fig. 28) at one or both ends (not always easy to see; mounting in Indian ink is useful, and essential for some). A hyaline (empty) cell, the primary appendage (fig. 28), may also be present. 48

- Spores without caudae, although a colourless gelatinous sheath may be present. Primary appendages present or absent. 88

48(47) Perithecia often hairy or tomentose when young. Immature spores long, wavy cylindrical, with a row of globules, and more likely to be seen than mature spores (fig. 29). Secondary appendages thin, simple, up to 60 × 3μm. Mature spores with a dark cell 14-25 × 7-13μm and pedicel (primary appendage) 25-50 × 3-6μm.

(*Cercophora*) 49

- Perithecia often with scales or setae at the neck or tomentose. Caudae, simple or compound. Immature spores clavate or ellipsoid, not long, wavy cylindrical. Mature spores readily observed. 51

49(48) Immature spores 45-70 × 4-6μm. 50

- Immature spores smaller, 38-52 × 3-3.5μm. Mature spores with upper (dark) cell 14-18 × 7-9μm; hyaline pedicel 27-36 × 3-3.5μm.

Cercophora silvatica

50(49) Perithecia with white or grey tomentum. Young spores 45-65 × 4.5-6μm. Mature spores with upper cell 17-25 × 8.5-13μm and pedicel 30-50μm long.

Cercophora coprophila (fig. 29)

\- Perithecia with flexuose brown hairs and, at the neck, tufts of agglutinated, swollen, obtuse hairs. Young Spores 52-68 × 4-5μm. Mature spores with upper cell 15-25 × 9-11μm and pedicel 35-45μm long.

Cercophora mirabilis

51(48) Primary appendage absent.

(*Arnium*, fig. 28) 52

\- Primary appendage present.   60

52(51) Asci (64-)128-spored. Spores 18-26 × (10)12-15μm. Perithecial neck sometimes with rigid, brown, septate hairs up to 330μm.

Arnium leporinum

\- Asci 4- or 8-spored.   53

53(52) Asci 4-spored.   54

\- Asci 8-spored.   55

54(53) Spores ellipsoid, sometimes inequilaterally flattened, 44-54 × 22-30μm, with 1 apical germ pore, caudae not swelling in water. Perithecium usually with lateral tufts of agglutinated hairs up to 550μm long.

Arnium arizonense

59

\-   Spores evenly ellipsoid-fusiform, 31-55 × 18-
           25μm, with germ pore at each end, caudae
           covering germ pores, 35-60 × 7-11μm, but
           rupturing and swelling to up to 130 ×
           50μm, and becoming diffuse and irregular.
           Perithecial neck covered with rigid hairs up
           to 190 × 2.5μm.

                                              Arnium hirtum

55(53)   Perithecial neck distinctly setose with rigid
         hairs.   56

\-   Perithecial neck without setae.   57

56(55)   Spores evenly ellipsoid-fusiform, 31-55 × 18-
         25μm, with germ pore at each end, caudae
         covering germ pores, 35-60 × 7-11μm, but
         rupturing and swelling up to 130 × 50μm,
         and becoming diffuse and irregular.
         Perithecial neck covered with rigid hairs up
         to 190 × 2.5μm.

                                              Arnium hirtum

\-   Spores slightly inequilateral, 35-43 × 17-
           23μm, caudae 50-75 × 5-8μm, not covering
           germ pores. Perithecial neck with brown
           hairs up to 250μm long.

                                            Arnium cervinum

57(55)   Perithecia covered with a dense tomentum
         of septate flexuous hairs. Spores mostly
         longer than 45μm. Only occasionally
         fimicolous.   58

\-   Perithecia without a tomentum. Spores up

to 45µm.   59

58(57)   Spores (40)45-54 × 25-35µm, uniseriate.
         Tomentum pale or grayish.
                                          Arnium olerum

-        Spores 47-70 x 20-30µm, biseriate above.
         Tomentum olivaceous brown.
                                      Arnium tomentosum

59(57)   Spores somewhat inequilateral, rounded
         below, pointed above, 31-40 × 18-24µm,
         caudae 50-120 × 6-10µm, with 1 apical germ
         pore not covered by cauda.
                                      Arnium caballinum

-        Spores equilateral, 36-44 × 20-23µm, caudae
         50-80 × 6-8µm, covering germ pores.
                                        Arnium mendax

60(51)   Perithecia with scales at the neck,
         composed of inflated and agglutinated cells
         (fig. 27, *S. conicum*).
                                    (*Schizothecium*) 61

-        Perithecia setose or hairy at the neck, but
         not with inflated cells, or neck black but
         almost hairless.
                                        (*Podospora*) 70

61(60)   Asci 4-spored.   62
-        Asci 8-spored.   63

62(61)   Spores 11-14.5 × 6.5-9µm.

		Schizothecium nanum (fig. 28)
-	Spores 19-24 × 12-14.5μm.	*Schizothecium tetrasporum*

63(61) Spores more than 30μm long.   64

-       Spores less than 30μm long.   65

64(63) Perithecia crowned with a fascicle of long
        agglutinated hairs at the neck, up to
        335μm long. Spores 31-40 × 15-25μm,
        biseriate.

                                        Schizothecium aloides

-       Perithecia with shorter, less remarkable
        tufts. Spores 30-45 × 19-24μm, ± uniseriate.
                                     Schizothecium glutinans

65(63) Perithecial neck with rigid setae, as well as
        agglutinated hairs (which may be greatly
        reduced). Asci 140-210 × 19-25μm, broadest
        at the markedly rounded apex. Spores 18-
        23 × 11-14μm.

                                     Schizothecium pilosum

-       Perithecial neck without rigid setae. Asci
        broadest in the middle.   66

66(65) Spores mostly over 23μm long.   67

-       Spores up to 23μm long.   69

67(66) Spores 22-25(27) × 11-13μm. Scales at neck
        distinct.

                                   Schizothecium hispidulum

-       Spores wider, 12-19μm   68

68(67) Perithecia 0.5-1mm high, scales at neck
        usually well developed. Spores (23)26-30 ×
        12-17μm.
                         Schizothecium conicum (fig. 27)

-       Perithecia 1-2mm diam., subpyriform, neck
        velvety with indistinct scales. Spores 24-28
        × 15-19μm.
                         Schizothecium squamulosum

69(66) Spores 17-23 × 8.5-13.5μm, primary
        appendage slender cylindrical, 6-8 × 2μm.
        Perithecia 0.25-0.7mm high, sometimes
        with poorly developed scales.
                         Schizothecium vesticola (fig. 28)

-       Spores 11-14 × 6-8μm, primary appendage
        short, 2μm long, almost triangular.
        Perithecia 0.3-0.45mm high, with short
        agglutinated hairs.
                         Schizothecium cervinum

        Asci 4-spored. Spores 35-40 ×   *Podospora*
70(60) 18-19μm.   *pauciseta*

-       Asci with more than 4 spores.   71

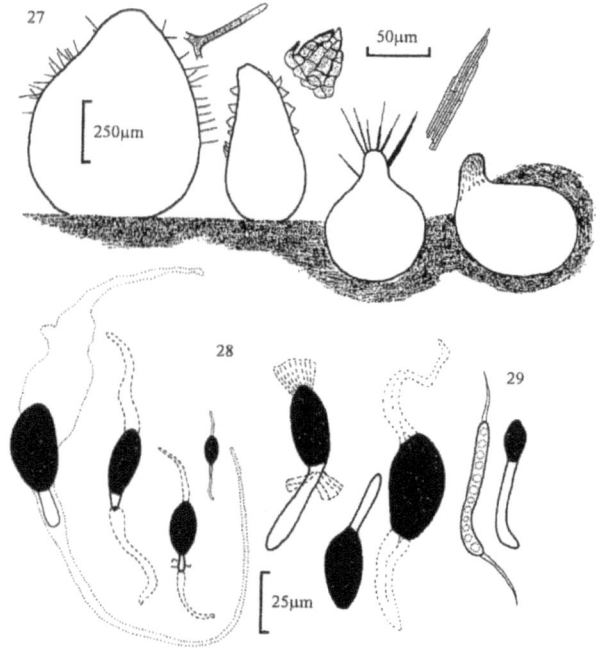

Fig. 27. Perithecia, from left, of *Podospora appendiculata*, *Schizothecium conicum*, *P. excentrica* and *P. decipiens*, with detail of hairs.

Fig. 28. Ascospores of, from left, *Podospora excentrica*, *P. appendiculata*, *S. vesticola*, *S. nanum*, *P. decipiens*, '*P. dagobertii*' and *Arnium* sp.

Fig. 29. *Cercophora coprophila*, immature (l) and mature (r) ascospores.

71(70)	Asci 8-spored.	72
-	Asci with more than 8 spores.	82
72(71)	Spores more than 45μm long.	73
-	Spores less than 45μm long.	74

73(72)   Spores 48-60 × 27-31µm, caudae apparently
         striate. Perithecia superficial, covered with
         rigid, nonagglutinated hairs up to 120µm.
                                    Podospora fimiseda

-        Spores 50-68 × 22-32µm, caudae apparently
         segmented, with an intestine-like
         appearance. Perithecia immersed to
         superficial, with a long neck, tomentose
         with long flexuous hairs when young,
         more or less glabrous when mature.
                                  Podospora intestinacea

74(72)   Perithecia superficial, ovoid to globose,
         covered with short (up to 100µm), sparse,
         radiating, hyaline tipped, hairs. Spores 24-
         31 × 11-15µm, with simple caudae.
                      Podospora appendiculata (figs 27, 28)

-        Perithecia with base immersed in substrate,
         pyriform, without such hairs.   75

75(74)   Perithecial neck with short tubercular
         hairs, up to 20µm long. Spores 32-42 × 17-
         22µm, with a long but withering primary
         appendage. Caudae in two rings, one
         inserted near the base of the primary
         appendage, the other at the spore apex. The
         individual filaments may be free, but often
         clump together to form an apparently
         broad appendage.
                          Podospora decipiens (figs 27, 28)

-        Perithecial hairs longer. Caudae single or 4
         at each end.   76

76(75) Spores with 4 caudae at each end. 77

\- Spores with a single cauda at each end. 78

77(76) Spores 40-45 × 22-25μm. *Podospora gwynne-vaughaniae*

\- Spores 29-40 × 16-25μm. *Podospora communis*

78(76) Spores less than 30 × 15μm. 79

\- Spores larger than 30 × 15μm. 80

79(78) Spores 21-28 × 11-14μm, primary appendage 12-14 × 4μm. Perithecia 0.3-0.5mm diam., neck setose with rigid cylindrical hairs. Asci 200-250 × 22-26μm, broadest in the middle.

Podospora ellisiana

\- Spores 18-23 × 11-14μm, primary appendage 4-8 × 3μm. Perithecia 0.2-0.3mm diam., neck setose with rigid hairs. Asci 140-210 × 19-25μm, broadest at the markedly rounded apex.

Schizothecium pilosum

80(78) Perithecia *ca* O.9-1.4mm high × 0.6-0.7(0.85)mm diam., neck not hairy. Spores (29)36-45 × (17.5)22-27μm, caudae ephemeral and difficult to see, even in Indian ink.

Podospora pyriformis

\- Perithecial neck with tufts of rigid hairs. 81

81(80) Perithecia 0.38-0.53mm high × 0.21-0.38mm diam., ± immersed, with hairs at the neck up to 335μm long, grouped in rigid fascicles. Spores slightly flattened on one side, 30-37 × 18-24μm, caudae invisible in water.

Podospora excentrica (figs 27, 28)

- Perithecia *ca* 0.8-1.4mm high × 0.4-0.7mm diam., semi-immersed, hairy all over, flexuous below, rigid and pointed at the neck up to 170μm. Spores 33-45 × 22-27μm.

Podospora perplexens

82(71) Asci 16-32-spored. Perithecial neck with short tubercular hairs. Spores 25-36 × 15-24μm. Caudae in two rings, one inserted at the base of the primary appendage, the other at the spore apex; individual filaments may be separate or clumped to appear as a broad single appendage (cf. *P. decipiens*).

Podospora pleiospora

- Asci with more than 32 spores. 83

83(82) Perithecia with tufts of rigid hairs at neck. Asci with more than 64 spores. 84

- Perithecia without tufts of rigid hairs. Asci 64-spored. 87

84(83) Spores 14-17 × 9-11μm. Asci 256-spored. Perithecia *ca* 500μm diam., immersed, except for the neck, which has tapered tufts of hairs up to 300μm.

Podospora curvicolla

-       Spores larger. Perithecia semi-immersed.   85

85(84) Spores (18)20-26 × 12-16μm, caudae of 2-
        several filaments covered with granules.
        Asci 512-spored. Perithecia up to 1mm high
        × 0.95mm diam., neck with rigid but non-
        agglutinated hairs up to 130μm long.

Podospora granulostriata

-       Caudae simple, without granular
        appearance. Asci 128-spored. Perithecia not
        larger than 750μm high × 500μm diam.,
        with rigid, non-agglutinated hairs up to
        190μm long at neck.   86

86(85) Spores 17-19 × 10-12μm.   *Podospora setosa*

-       Spores 19-24 × 11-16μm.   *Podospora tarvisina*
        (See discussion in Lundqvist (1972) on
        these last three names)

87(83) Spores 24-34 × 14-19μm, caudae in two
        rings, one inserted at the base of the
        primary appendage, the other at the spore
        apex; individual filaments may be separate
        or clumped to appear as a broad single
        appendage (cf. *P. decipiens/P. pleiospora*).
        Perithecia *ca* 0.6-1.1mm high × 0.4-0.5mm
        diam., covered with flexuous hairs or
        rarely smooth.

Podospora myriaspora

-       Spores 15-20 × 10-15μm, caudae small,

simple and evanescent. Perithecia 0.4-
0.5mm high, covered with long flexuous
hairs.

Podospora collapsa

88(47) Spores with primary appendage.   89

-       Spores without primary appendage.   93

89(88) Spores with primary appendage directed
        towards base of ascus.   90

-       Spores with primary appendage directed
        towards apex of ascus.

                                          (*Anopodium*) 91

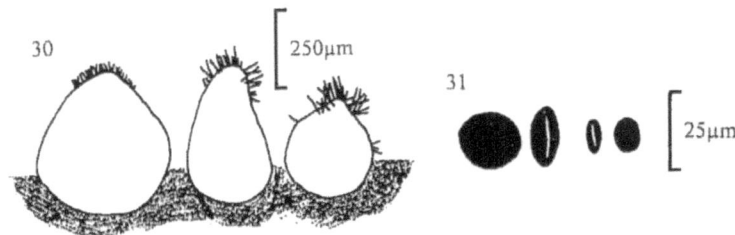

Fig. 30.. Perithecia of, from left, *Coniochaeta ligniaria, C. scatigena* and *C. hansenii.*

Fig. 31.. Ascospores of *C. scatigena* (l) and *C. ligniaria* (r).

90(89) Spores 34-45 × 19-25μm, without caudae
        but surrounded by a thin (*ca* 5μm)
        gelatinous sheath. Perithecia *ca* 0.5-0.7mm
        diam., ± smooth.

                                        Podospora globosa

-       Spores 17-20 × 8-9.5μm, flattened on one
        side, convex on the other. Perithecia 0.3-
        0.45μm diam., with distal cells of

agglutinated hairs fimbriate.

Podospora fimbriata

91(89) Perithecia hairy. Spores 27-32 × 16-19µm, appendage 15-18 × 2.5-3µm.

Anopodium ampullaceum

- Perithecia glabrous.   92

92(91) Spores 28-32 × 16-21µm, appendage 12-15 × 3-3.8µm.

Anopodium epile

- Spores 30-37 × 16-20µm, appendage 24-27 × 5µm.

'Podospora' dagobertii (fig. 28)

(The combination in *Anopodium* has not been made; see Lundqvist, 1964, 1972)

93(88) Spores flattened, disc shaped, with a germ slit around the edge. Perithecial neck with short (up to 120µm) setae.

(*Coniochaeta*, figs 30, 31) 94

- Spores ellipsoid. Perithecial neck without setae or with very prominent (up to 950µm) tufts of agglutinated hairs.   99

94(93) Asci with numerous (64-128) spores.   95

- Asci 8-spored.   96

95(94) Spores 6-10 × 5-9 × 4-7µm. Perithecial setae up to 120µm long.

Coniochaeta hansenii (fig. 30)

-        Spores 13-16 × 9.5-13.5 × 5.5-8µm.
         Perithecial setae up to 35µm long.

                                                    Coniochaeta sp.

96(94)   Spores 7-9 × 6-8 × 5-6µm, slightly flattened.
                                              Coniochaeta leucoplaca

-        Spores larger.   97

97(96)   Spores narrowly elliptical in face view
         (length more than 2 × width), *ca* 13-18 × 6-9
         × 4-6µm.
                                              Coniochaeta saccardoi

-        Spores broadly elliptical to nearly circular
         in face view (length less than 2 × width).   98

98(97)   Spores (9)10-16(20) × 7.5-10(15) × (4)5-
         8µm. Neck setae 20-50µm long.
                                     Coniochaeta ligniaria (figs 30, 31)

-        Spores (16)17-23 × (10)13-19 × 7.5-
         10(15)µm. Neck setae 40-80µm long.
                                     Coniochaeta scatigena (figs 30, 31)

99(93)   Perithecial neck with prominent
         agglutinated tufts of rigid setae up to
         950µm long. Spores 43-54 × 20-29µm,
         with apical germ pore. A gelatinous
         sheath which surrounds the whole spore
         swells in water, and appears fringed at
         the margin and radially striate.
                                        Arnium macrothecium

-        Perithecial neck without setae.

Gelatinous sheaths may be clearly visible around spores, but are not complex in structure. 100

100(99) Spores with germ slit along the side. Ascus with a large and complex plug at the tip staining blue or red in KI (other genera have asci with blue staining ascus tips, but the feature is very pronounced in this genus and is unlikely to be mistaken). Perithecia form singly or severally in a stroma which is usually of limited extent, often without a definite margin. [N.B. if orange and with a stroma see *Selinia*, 119].

(*Hypocopra*, fig. 32) 101

- Spores without germ slits, but often asymmetrical, and with a small papilla at the basal end. Asci without complex apical plug.

(*Sordaria*, fig. 33) 107

101(100) Spores mostly less than 25μm long. 102
- Spores more than 25μm long. 104

102(101) Spores 9-14 × 6-7μm.   *Hypocopra parvula*
- Spores larger. 103

103(102) Stroma with a brown hyphal mat between perithecial necks. Spores 19-27 × 10-14μm.

Hypocopra equorum (fig. 32)

-	Stroma with white hyphae between black perithecial necks, becoming smooth. Spores 23-25 × 12-14µm.	
		Hypocopra brefeldii

104(101)	Ascospores up to 15µm wide.	105
-	Ascospores 15µm or wider.	106

105(104)	Ascospores 25-31 × 10-15µm, distinctly flattened on one side. Ascus plug blue in KI, but becoming reddish.	
		Hypocopra planispora
-	Ascospores 26-32 × 13-14µm, ellipsoid and narrowed towards their ends.	
		Hypocopra stephanophora

106(104)	Ascospores 27-43 × 16-20µm.	*Hypocopra merdaria*
-	Ascospores 38-50 × 19-24µm.	*Hypocopra stercoraria*

107(100)	Spores up to 10µm long.	108
-	Spores 10µm or longer.	109

108(107)	Asci 8-spored. Spores 8 × 4µm.	*Sordaria minima*
-	Asci *ca* 128-spored. Spores 5-8 × 4-5µm.	
		Sordaria polyspora

109(107)	Spores relatively narrow, at least twice as long as wide, 22-26 × 9-12µm. Gelatinous sheath broad, distinct.	

Sordaria alcina

-         Spores relatively broad, less than twice as long as wide.   110

110(109)   Spores mostly 25μm or longer.   111

-         Spores up to 25μm long.   112

111(110)   Spores (21)23-29(30) × 14.5-17(18)μm, with apiculate base. Gelatinous sheath broad, distinct. Asci 240-300 × 20-24μm.

Sordaria superba

-         Spores (26)28-35 × (17)18-22μm, with slightly apiculate base. Gelatinous sheath broad, distinct. Asci 280-350 × 30-35μm.

Sordaria macrospora

112(110)   ISpores with gelatinous sheath absent or very thin, 19.5-25 × 15.5-19μm.

Sordaria humana (fig. 33)

-         Spores with gelatinous sheath, up to 15μm diam.   113

113(112)   Spores obovoid to broadly ellipsoid, 18-23 × 12-15μm.

Sordaria lappae

-         Spores ellipsoid, 17-25 × 10-14μm.

Sordaria fimicola (fig. 33)

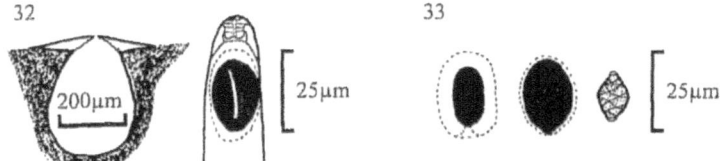

Fig. 32. *Hypocopra equorum*, perithecium with limited stroma, and detail of ascus tip with blue staining plug and spore.
Fig. 33. Ascospores, from left, of *Sordaria fimicola, S. humana* and *Sphaerodes fimicola*.

114(3)   Spores 20-28 × 12-16μm, with subacute
ends, each with a germ pore.

Gelasinospora adjuncta

-    Spores larger.   115

115(114)   Asci 4-spored. Spores 24-29 × 15-18μm,
with rounded ends and one germ pore.

Gelasinospora tetrasperma

-    Asci 8-spored. Spores 26-35 ×   *Gelasinospora*
22-27μm   *cerealis*

116(4)   Perithecia orange to golden, often
gregarious, almost spherical, necks *ca*
50μm diam., 15μm high, setae at ostiole
hyaline, up to 35 × 3μm. Spores
limoniform, with a germ pore at each
end, 15-25 × 9-16μm.

Sphaerodes fimicola (fig. 33)

-    Perithecia yellow or reddish brown
(darker when filled with mature spores),
neck 50μm long, with setae at the ostiole
40-70μm long. Spores dark brown to

black, limoniform, 20-34 × 11-17μm, with
apical germ pore.

Melanospora brevirostris

117(2)   Asci more than 8-spored.   see Key 1 at 86

\-   Asci with 8 or fewer spores, or asci
evanescent, not readily observed.   118

118(117)   Perithecia orange/yellow, 500-1000μm
diam. Spores long (over 45μm) or 2-
celled if shorter.   119

\-   Perithecia smaller, or black or with a
neck. Spores shorter (less than 20μm) or
septate if longer.   120

119(118)   Perithecia orange, 500-1000μm diam., in
small groups on a limited stroma. Spores
thick walled, 48-60 × 22-26μm, with a
gelatinous sheath.

Selinia pulchra

\-   Perithecia orange yellow, superficial, *ca*
500μm diam., with ostiole in a disc
surrounded by silvery triangular tufts of
hyphae *ca* 100μm long. Spores ellipsoid,
1-septate, 12-14 × 4-5μm.

Nectria suffulta

120(118)   Perithecia reddish brown or pale,
hyaline, with a distinct neck.   121

\-   Perithecia black.   131

121(120)   Perithecia globose, up to 250µm diam.,
           immersed, reddish brown, with a neck 1-
           3 mm long. Asci broad ellipsoid, 5-
           8.5µm, rapidly breaking down and
           difficult to see. Spores ellipsoid-allantoid.
           5.5-7 × 1.5-2µm, collecting in a pearly
           droplet at the fringed tip of the
           perithecial beak.

                         Viennotidia fimicola (fig. 34)

-          Perithecia pyriform, very pale in colour,
           60-200µm diam., with a neck 60-700µm
           long. Asci rarely visible. Spores pointed-
           fusiform, 1-3 septate, often with a sheath
           and clumped together in fascicles.

                              (*Pyxidiophora*, fig. 36) 122

122(121)   Neck 95-145µm long, brown, rugose,
           with cells arranged in 5-6 longitudinal
           rows visible in one view. Spores 38-52µm
           long.

                              Pyxidiophora badiorostris

-          Neck not brown or rugose, composed of
           hyaline, irregularly arranged cylindrical
           cells.   123

123(122)   Spores less than 45µm long.   124

-          Spores more than 45µm long.   125

124(123)   Spores 35-45µm long, with brown apical
           or subapical patches of pigment.

                           Pyxidiophora brunneocapitatus

-          Spores 35-43µm long, without brown

                              77

apical or subapical patches of pigment.

Pyxidiophora microsporus

125(123)   Spores mostly 45-60μm long.   126

-            Spores mostly longer than 60μm.   129

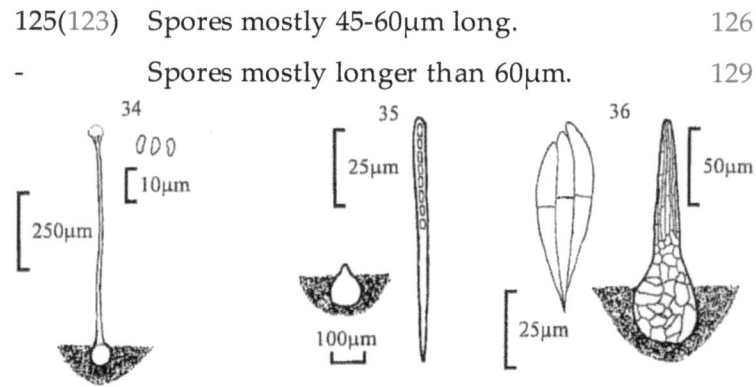

Fig. 34. *Viennotidia fimicola*, perithecium and spores.
Fig. 35. *Phomatospora coprophila*, perithecium, and ascus with spores.
Fig. 36. *Pyxidiophora petchii*, perithecium and spores.

126(125)   Perithecia 70-100μm diam., neck 100-
             190μm long. Spores (43)48-58(65)μm
             long.

Pyxidiophora grovei

-            Perithecia usually less than 80μm diam.   127

127(126)   Perithecial necks mostly less than 100μm
             long. Spores (45)48-57(60)μm long.

Pyxidiophora arvernensis

-            Perithecial necks up to 200μm long.   128

128(127)   Spores 45-53μm long.

Pyxidiophora petchii (fig. 36)

-            Spores 53-65μm   *Pyxidiophora*

long.   *schotterianus*

129(125)   Spores 60-70µm long.   130

\-   Spores (75)80-90(100)µm. Perithecia 120-160µm diam., neck 220-370µm long.
                Pyxidiophora bainemensis

130(129)   Perithecial necks 300-700µm long. Spores 60-70µm. Perithecia 100-120µm diam.
                Pyxidiophora spinuliformis

\-   Perithecial necks 225-265µm long. Spores 65-70µm. Perithecia 110-125µm diam.
                Pyxidiophora marchalii

131(120)   Perithecia small, up to 400µm diam., with hairy necks. Spores hyaline or pale, coppery-red en masse, extruded in tendrils.   132

\-   Perithecia larger, without hairy necks. If smaller than 200µm, with spores smaller than 5 × 3µm.   134

132(131)   Spores reniform, with gelatinous sheath, 3.5 × 2-3µm, yellow, reddish brown *en masse* in extruded tendrils. Asci spherical, evanescent. Perithecia black, spherical, 200-400µm diam., with cylindrical neck up to 300µm long, with sparse pointed hairs.
                Microascus longirostris

\-   Spores larger, not reniform. Perithecia up

to 300µm diam. 133

133(132) Perithecial necks long, up to 750µm,
with terminal hairs up to 1500µm,
curved or circinate at tips. Spores
limoniform, 7-10.5 × 5.5-7µm.

Lophotrichus ampullus

- Perithecial necks short, *ca* 50µm, with
long straight tapering hairs. Spore shape
limoniform/variable, 6-7.5 × 5-5.5µm,
with prominent germ pores.

Lophotrichus bartletti

134(131) Perithecia up to 150µm diam., immersed
but for a conical neck 50-75µm high.
Asci 50 × 2-2.5µm. Spores minute,
cylindrical, 3.5-4.5 × 1.75-2.5µm.

Phomatospora coprophila (fig. 35)

- Perithecia more obvious, often hairy, or
tomentose when young. Immature
spores up to 70µm long, wavy
cylindrical, with a row of globules inside
and a short thin appendage at each end.

(see *Cercophora*, 49)

135(1) Perithecia immersed, surrounded at the
neck by a very limited flange-like stroma
which is easily overlooked.

see *Hypocopra*, 101

or if orange see *Selinia*, 119

- Stroma very conspicuous. 136

136(135)   Perithecia in a subglobose group at the
           tip of the stromatic stalk. Spores with
           germ slit and gelatinous sheath.

                                    (*Podosordaria*) 137

-          Perithecia not in a terminal head.   139

137(136)   Stalk short, 3-5mm. Spores (12)14-19 × 6-
           9μm, slightly flattened on one side.

                                    Podosordaria leporina

-          Stalk long, 1-6cm. Spores larger.   138

138(137)   Spores 21-24 × 11-12μm. Stromatic stalk
           hairy.

                                    Podosordaria tulasnei

-          Spores 40-60 × 20-30μm. Stromatic stalk
           not hairy.

                                    Podosordaria pedunculata

139(136)   Stroma externally black, rooted or
           partially immersed in the dung,
           expanding at the surface to form a white
           disc up to 15mm diam., punctate with
           black perithecial ostioles.

                                    (*Poronia*) 140

-          Stroma not as above.   141

140(139)   Spores 18-26 × 7-12μm, bean shaped,
           with gelatinous sheath. Stroma deeply
           rooted. Especially on horse dung.

                                    Poronia punctata

-          Spores (22)25-32(35) × (12)14-18μm,

81

oblong ellipsoid to slightly fusiform.
Stroma not deeply rooted. Especially on
rabbit dung near the sea.

Poronia erici

141(139)   Stroma spreading over surface of dung
           or filamentous. Spores ellipsoid to
           slightly flattened on one side, with germ
           slit. (Xerophilic fungi developing after
           long periods of relatively dry
           incubation).

(*Wawelia*) 142

-          Stroma clavate, black, partly immersed to
           superficial, usually aggregated in small
           groups, *ca* 1-1.5mm high × 0.6-0.7mm
           diam., each containing a single
           perithecium. Spores ellipsoid with germ
           pore and gelatinous sheath.

(*Bombardioidea*) 146

142(141)   Stroma spreading on substrate, black
           brown, firm but not brittle. Ascomata
           globose, 0.5-1mm, with white hyphae at
           neck. Spores broad limoniform, 15-19 ×
           9-10μm.

Wawelia effusa

-          Perithecia globose to pyriform, black,
           brown or dark grey, produced laterally
           along the length of fine stromatal
           strands growing from the dung.   143

143(142)   Asci 4-spored.   144

82

-          Asci 8-spored.

144(143)   Spores 15-18 × 9-12µm. Perithecia up to
           400µm diam., dark grey at maturity,
           single or clustered, the ostiole with a
           crown of silvery white hyphae. Stromata
           up to 30 × 0.1-0.5mm.

                                                   Wawelia sp.

-          Spores 6-8 × 4-6µm. Stromata conical,
           white, 5-12 × 1-2mm.

                                                   Wawelia regia

145(143)   Perithecia hairy, globose, 350-500µm
           diam., stromatal strands up to 25mm
           long. Spores ellipsoid, flattened on one
           side, 9-12 × 6-8µm.

                                                Wawelia octospora

-          Perithecia villose with conidiophores,
           globose, 230-420µm diam., produced
           laterally on stromatic filaments 20-30 ×
           0.1-0.3mm. Filaments pink at first, with a
           white pointed tip, becoming brown,
           velvety with conidiophores. Spores
           ellipsoid to flattened on one side, 7.5-9.5
           × 3-4.5µm.

                                           Wawelia sp. (fig. 37)

Fig. 37. *Wawelia* sp., stromatic filaments with perithecia growing from a rabbit pellet, ascospores, and conidiophore and conidia.

146(141)	Asci 8-spored. Spores 20-31 × 9.5-15µm.
	Bombardioidea bombardioides
-	Asci 4-spored. 147

147(146)   Spores 24-34 × 15-19(20)µm. Basal germ
pore less distinct than the apical one.
Bombardioidea serignanensis

-   Spores 34-43 × 16-22µm. Distinct germ
pore at each end of spore.
Bombardioidea stercoris

148
(key
1,1)   Fruit bodies solitary or in small groups,
each a subglobose, fertile, light brown
head on a slender sterile stalk. Head soon
bursting to expose the yellow
ochraceous spore mass. On mixtures of
bird droppings, cast pellets and decaying
animal material.   149

-   Fruit bodies superficial, lacking a distinct
stalk.   150

149(148) Spores 5-8 × 2-3μm. Head 1-2mm diam.
          Onygena corvina (fig. 38)

-         Spores 7-9 × 4-6μm, 4-5μm. Head   *Onygena*
          2-4mm diam.   *equina*

150(148) Fruit bodies with an external wall of
          loosely anastomosing and interwoven
          hyphae, and with ± specialised terminal
          cells (**gymnothecia**, fig. 39).   151

-         Fruit bodies with a well defined
          parenchymatic wall (**cleistothecia**, fig.
          46).   161

151(150) Gymnothecia with simple thin-walled, ±
          uniform and poorly developed hyphae
          constituting the outer hyphal sheath.   152

-         Gymnothecia with thick-walled hyphae
          modified at their ends into appendages,
          or if thin-walled then always
          accompanied by appendages (i.e. curled,
          toothed or pointed hyphae).   155

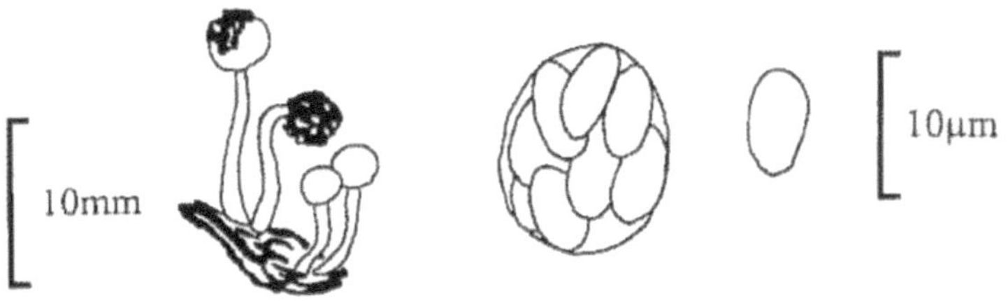

Fig. 38. *Onygena corvina*, habit sketch, ascus and ascospore.

152(151) Gymnothecia red-orange to brick-red.

85

Ascospores orange, subglobose to
ellipsoid, with an equatorial furrow,
smooth, 4.5-5.5 × 3.5-4.5µm.

Arachniotus ruber (fig. 40)

- Gymnothecia white or yellow, never
orange or brick-red. Ascospores without
an equatorial furrow.   153

153(152) Gymnothecia white. Ascospores hyaline,
ellipsoid, smooth, 3-4 × 2-2.5µm.

Arachniotus candidus

- Gymnothecia distinctly pigmented,
yellow or brown. Ascospores larger than
4µm.   154

154(153) Gymnothecia yellow brown. Ascospores
orange to brownish, slightly lenticular,
smooth or slightly roughened, 5-6.5 ×
3.3-4.6µm.

Arachniotus confluens

- Gymnothecia lemon yellow. Ascospores
lemon yellow, lenticular, smooth, 5-6 × 3-
4.5µm.

Arachniotus citrinus

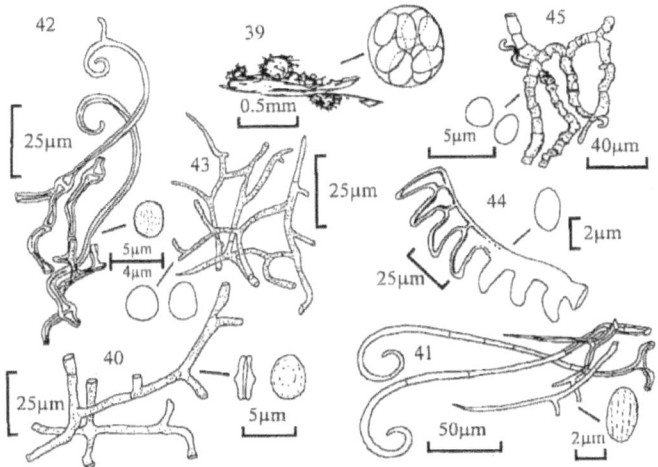

Fig. 39. Habit sketch of a gymnothecium and ascus.
Figs 40-45. Spores and peridial hyphae.
Fig. 40. *Arachniotus ruber.* **Fig. 41.** *Myxotrichum chartarum.*
Fig. 42. *Gymnoascus californiensis.* **Fig. 43.** *Gymnoascus reesii.*
Fig. 44. *Ctenomyces serratus.* **Fig. 45.** *Arthroderma curreyi.*

155(151)   Gymnothecia possessing only thick
           pigmented hyphae.   156

-          Gymnothecia possessing ± thin, hyaline
           hyphae with only a few, although often
           distinctive, appendages (i.e. comb-shaped
           end cells or dumb-bell shaped asperulate
           cells accompanying twisted and bent
           hyphae).   160

156(155)   Gymnothecia brown-black or dark
           greenish-grey, with external hyphae
           with spine-like branches and septate,
           hooked appendages. Ascospores orange
           brownish, ovate, delicately striate, 4-5.2 ×

2.4-3.3μm.

Myxotrichum chartarum (fig. 41)

- Gymnothecia never black, and, if possessing thick-walled hyphae, then appendages never septate. Ascospores smooth, or if ornamented then asperulate or echinulate.   157

157(156) Gymnothecia rose to orange-brown or yellowish. Appendages curved or irregularly branched and pointed, never verticillately branched. Ascospores smooth, or at most asperulate.   158

- Gymnothecia red-brown with appendages verticillately branched. Ascospores 3-4.5 × 2-2.8μm, yellowish brown, lenticular.

Actinodendron verticillatum

158(157) Gymnothecia rosy pink when young, becoming browner, with spines and curved, non-septate hairs. Ascospores hyaline, globose to subglobose, asperulate, 3-5 × 2.5-4μm.

Gymnoascus californiensis (fig. 42)

- Gymnothecia yellow. Ascospores smooth.   159

159(158) Gymnothecia yellow to yellow-brown, without elongated appendages but with thick-walled branches, few of which are pointed. Ascospores globose-ellipsoid, yellow to brownish, 3-4.5 × 3.5μm.

Gymnoascus reesii (fig. 43)

- Gymnothecia golden yellow to reddish-brown, with acute-ended appendages. Ascospores lenticular, smooth, hyaline, 2.5-3.5 × 2-2.5μm.

Pseudogymnoascus roseus

160(155) Gymnothecia orange brown, with comb-like appendages. Ascospores slightly lenticular, pale orange, 3.3-3.6 × 2-2.6μm.

Ctenomyces serratus (fig. 44)

- Gymnothecia whitish to pale ochraceous, particularly when dry, with few appendages but those present twisted and bent, and their branches constricted with regular or irregular dumb-bell shaped cells. Hyphal walls asperulate or with protuberances. Ascospores smooth, lenticular, hyaline, 2.4-3.3 × 2μm.

Arthroderma curreyi (fig. 45)

161(150) Asci relatively large, 100-200-spored, 1-3/fruit body. 'Cleistothecia' minute, <100 (rarely <250)μm diam., immersed.

see *Thelebolus* etc. (Key 1, 86)

- Asci with 8 or fewer spores.   162

162(161) Ascospores purple at maturity, large, 50-70 × 25-35μm, epispore with a few longitudinal cracks.

see *Ascobolus immersus* (Key 1, 48)

| - | Ascospores smaller, hyaline, yellow, olivaceous, brown or black. | 163 |

163(162)   Ascospores olivaceous, brown or black, at least in part.   164

| - | Ascospores aseptate, hyaline, yellow or other pale colours. | 174 |

164(163)   Ascospores 4-celled (cf. *Sporormiella*), with germ slits, readily fragmenting. Asci clavate, bitunicate. Cleistothecia black, shiny, up to 500μm diam.   165

| - | Ascospores 1- or 2-celled. | 166 |

165(164)   Ascus stalk up to 20μm long. Ascospores 25-32 × 5μm.

Preussia vulgaris

| - | Ascus stalk 30-60μm long. Ascospores 26-38 × 5-7μm. |

Preussia funiculata (fig. 47)

166(164)   Ascospores 2-celled.   167

| - | Ascospores 1-celled | 170 |

167(166)   Spores unequally 2-celled, one brown ellipsoid, with an apical germ pore, 10-12 × 6.5-7.5μm, the other a basal hyaline, cylindrical pedicel, 6-8 × 3μm. Cleistothecia black, globose, up to 250μm

diam., covered with flexuous brown
hairs up to 1mm long. Asci evanescent.

Zopfiella erostrata

\-   Spores equally 2-celled.   168

168(167)   Spores not constricted at the septum,
           ellipsoid, golden-brown, 25-30 × 10-15µm
           with 1-3 guttules in each cell.
           Cleistothecia gregarious on a mycelial
           mat, whitish to pale orange, up to
           500µm diam.

Heleococcum aurantiacum (fig. 48)

\-   Spores hyaline, divided into two almost
           globose cells by the constricting septum.
           Ascomata superficial, globose, dark
           coloured.

(*Mycoarachis*) 169

169(168)   Asci 8-spored, 5.5-11µm diam. Spores 5-
           5.5 × 3-3.5µm.

Mycoarachis inversa

\-   Asci 4-spored, 6-6.5µm diam. Spores 4.5-
           5 × 2-2.5µm.

Mycoarachis tetraspora

170(166)   Asci broad-clavate, (1)-2-(3)-spored, 30-50
           × 13-18µm. Spores brown-black with
           short ridges and warts, subglobose, 12-
           15.5 × 11-12.5µm, with a single germ
           pore.

Copromyces bisporus (fig. 49)

\-   Asci 8-spored.   171

91

171(170)   Spores globose, sooty brown, 3μm diam. Cleistothecia gregarious, with basal spirally coiled appendages, black, 100-200μm diam., partially immersed in a white to red felty hyphal mat.

Pleuroascus nicholsonii

-        Spores larger, ellipsoid or limoniform.   172

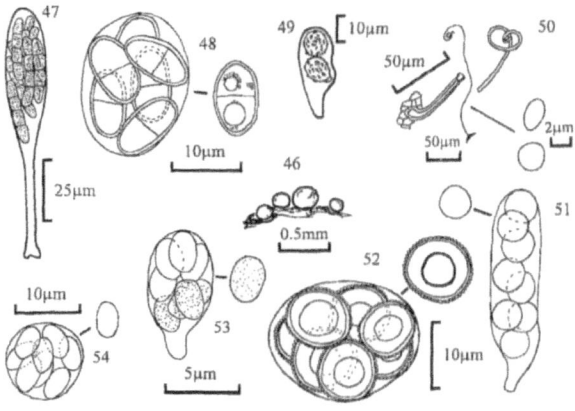

Fig. 46. Habit sketch of cleistothecia.
Figs 47-54. Asci and spores.
Fig. 47. *Preussia funiculata*.   Fig. 48. *Heleococcum aurantiacum*.
Fig. 49. *Copromyces bisporus*.   Fig. 50. *Arachnomyces nitidus*.
Fig. 51. *Orbicula parietina*.   Fig. 52. *Roumegueriella rufula*.
Fig. 53. *Aphanoascus stercoraria*.   Fig. 54. *Pseudeurotium ovale*.

172(171)   Spores olivaceous, limoniform, usually with an apical germ pore. Perithecia greyish or greenish, abundantly hairy, branched or simple, straight or curly. Asci pedicellate, soon disappearing.

see *Chaetomium* at 5

-        Spores darker, with 1 or more minute

92

germ pores. Cleistothecia distinctly but not abundantly hairy. 173

173(172)   Spores smoky brown, broadly ovoid, 9-14 × 6-9μm. Cleistothecial hairs short, up to 30μm.

Thielavia wareingii

\-   Spores dark brown, flattened limoniform, 13-16 × 10-13 × 8-9μm. Cleistothecial hairs of two types, some smooth, dark brown, arising from the base up to 3mm long, others greyish green, rough, up to *ca* 120μm.

Thielavia fimeti

174(163)   Cleistothecia produced within a common arachnoid mycelial mass. Spores smooth or minutely asperulate, yellow to yellow-brown, broadly ellipsoid, 4-5 × 3-5μm.

Aphanoascus fulvescens

\-   Cleistothecia single or gregarious, but not on or in a mycelial mass. 175

175(174)   Cleistothecia 170-750μm diam., covered with long (several mm when extended), thick-walled, aseptate, helical appendages. Asci clavate cylindrical, evanescent, 35-62 × 12-21μm. Spores ellipsoid, hyaline, 12-17 × 9-12μm.

Lasiobolidium spirale

\-   Cleistothecia without coiled appendages. 176

176(175) Cleistothecia with hairs or appendages.   177

\-   Cleistothecia smooth.   178

177(176) Cleistothecia black, shining, 100-200µm
          diam., with dark brown-black thick-
          walled hairs with hooked tips. Asci 8-
          15µm diam. Spores straw or copper
          coloured, ellipsoid, 4-7 × 3.5-4.5µm with
          de Bary bubble and a germ pore at each
          end.

                                        Kernia nitida

\-   Cleistothecia reddish brown, less than
          1mm diam., with long simple appendages
          curled at the tips. Spores hyaline, oblate,
          3.55 × 2-3µm.

                        Arachnomyces nitidus (fig. 50)

178(176) Ascospores globose, larger than 9µm.   179

\-   Ascospores ellipsoid, up to 9µm. Asci
          always subglobose.   180

179(178) Ascospores, smooth, 9-13µm.
                            Orbicula parietina (fig. 51)

\-   Ascospores ornamented, 13-24µm Asci
          subglobose. Cleistothecia ochraceous,
          becoming yellowish brown or flushed
          cinnamon.

                      Roumegueriella rufula (fig. 52)

180(178) Ascospores hyaline, then faintly yellowish,
          minutely spiny, 2.5-3 × 2-2.5µm. Cleistothecia

pale, then dark brown.

Aphanoascus stercoraria (fig. 53)

\-   Ascospores hyaline, then brown, smooth, 5.5-6
× 3.5-4µm. Cleistothecia dark brown from the
beginning.

Pseudeurotium ovale (fig. 54)

Key 3. Basidiomycota

1	Basidia single-celled (fig. 55).	2
\-	Basidia transversely or longitudinally septate (fig. 55), or difficult to observe.	71
2(1)	Fruit body agaricoid, i.e. mushroom-shaped with gills underneath cap (figs 56, 67).	3
\-	Fruit body not agaricoid, without gills (figs 65, 66).	69
3(2)	Spore print white or pale coloured, hyaline s.m. (Usually on straw/dung mixtures, never on raw dung except when very old).	5
\-	Spore print coloured.	4
4(3)	Spore print pinkish or pale cinnamon, honey-coloured s.m. (Usually on straw/dung mixtures, never on raw dung).	6
\-	Spore print darker, in shades of brown or black.	8

5(3) Stem eccentric. Fruit body pure white. Spores
      ellipsoid, smooth.

                              Pleurotellus s. lato

      (If gills pink and spores longitudinally ridged
      see *Clitopilus passackerianus*, fig. 67)

-     Stem central.   7

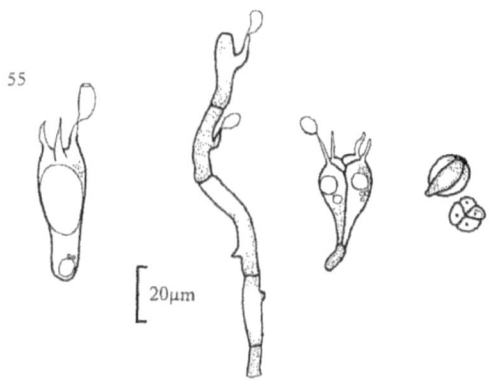

Fig. 55. From left, sketches of holobasidium, with
mature basidiospore showing germ pore;
auriculariaceous basidium; tremellaceous basidium,
lateral view and as often seen in sections.

6(4)   Fruit body white, ivory or very pale tan,
        with a smell of cucumber. Gills decurrent.

                              Clitocybe augeana

-       Fruit body yellow, with scaly cap. Gills free
        or just adnate. Fruit body with distinct
        ring and granular veil. (Commonly in
        plant pots. Probably associated with peaty
        material more than dung).

                              Leucocoprinus birnbaumii
        (*L. cœpaestipes* and *L. lilacinogranulosus* occur
        in similar situations).

7(5)   Fruit body with amethyst/purple shades,
        with eccentric stem. Spores subglobose,
        slightly ornamented to nearly smooth. (On
        compost heaps in gardens).

                                    Lepista nuda

-       Fruit body with pink gills and distinct
        volva at stem base. Cap white to pale hazel.
        Stem white. Spores broadly ellipsoid,
        smooth.

                                    Volvariella speciosa

8(4)   Spore print distinctly brown (fulvous,
        tawny, rust coloured etc.).   9

-       Spore print some darker shade, fuscous,
        fuliginous or violaceous black.   20

        Stem distinctly annulate, apex   *Conocybe*
9(8)   striate.   *percincta*
        (Has been found on straw/dung mixtures,
        never on raw dung).

-       Stem lacking a veil.   10

10(9)   Cap rich chrome yellow, viscid, soon
        reduced to a sticky mass, easily collapsing.
                                    Bolbitius vitellinus

-       Cap in shades of brown, never brightly
        coloured and if collapsing then cap
        elongate-cylindric and white to pale cream.   11

11(10) Spore print dull, sepia or snuff-brown. On
        rabbit pellets in sand dunes.
                                    Agrocybe subpediades

-         Spore print, brighter coloured, orange/rust
          brown.

                                        (*Conocybe*) 12

12(11)   Gill edge with irregularly fusoid cystidia
          with obtuse apices (lageniform). Cap viscid.
                                        Conocybe coprophila

-         Gill edge with distinctly capitate cells
          resembling a glass stoppered bottle
          (lecythiform). Cap never viscid, often
          pubescent under a lens.   13

13(12)   Stem covered in long hairs.   14

-         Stem covered in lecythiform cells similar to
          those on gill edge, giving a farinaceous
          appearance under a lens. NEVER with long
          hairs. (Dung/straw mixtures). Large as in a
          Cortinarius. Spores smooth.
                                        Conocybe intrusa
          (*C. leucopus* has been found on manured
          soil in gardens; *C. antipus* has hexagonal
          spores and grows on dung piles).

14(13)   Stem with both long hairs and lecythiform
          cystidia.
                                                         15

-         Stem with hairs and lageniform cystidia.
                                                         16

15(14)   Spores 11-14 × 7-9μm. Taste and smell
          strong, of fresh meal.
                                        Conocybe farinacea

98

\-   Spores large, over 15 × up to 10μm. Taste
      and smell none or slightly acidic.
                              Conocybe pubescens
      (*C. subpubescens* might be found on
      straw/dung mixtures, and differs in spores
      11-13 × 6-8μm).

16(14) Basidia 2-spored.   *Conocybe rickenii*

\-   Basidia 4-spored.   17

17(16) Spores ellipsoid.   18

\-   Spores lentiform, angular in   *Conocybe*
        face view.   *lenticulospora*

18(17) Cap grey, contrasting with yellowish cream
        gills and pale stem. Spores 10.5-12.5 × 6-
        7μm.
                              Conocybe murinacea

\-   Cap pinkish brown or tawny.   19

19(18) Spores 11-12 × 7.2-7.8μm. Cap sienna. On
        raw dung.
                              Conocybe fimetaria

\-   Spores 10-12 × 6-7μm. Cap pinkish to
        cinnamon brown. On manured soil or
        sewage sludge.
                        Conocybe fuscomarginata
        (*Conocybe siennophylla* might be found on
        straw/dung mixtures or in soil in
        greenhouses. It differs in having smaller
        spores).

20(8)	Cap deliquescing to some degree at maturity. Basidia of 2 or 3 different sizes.	
		(*Coprinus*) 21
-	Cap not deliquescing. Basidia of one size only.	49
21(20)	Veil on cap absent, cap either covered with small hairs (setules) or naked.	22
-	Cap covered with a granular, micaceous, powdery or fibrillar veil.	28

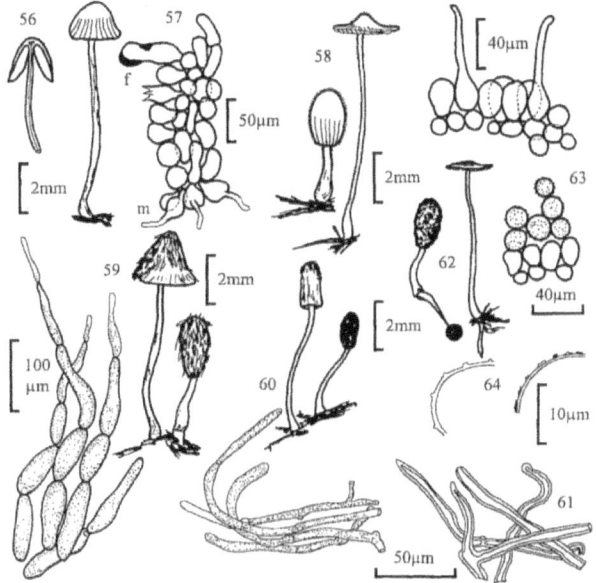

Fig. 56. Habit sketch of a stipitate agaric, *Psathyrella stercoraria*, with section.

Fig. 57. Sketch of gill section of *Psathyrella* sp., showing position of marginal (m) and facial (f) cystidia.

Fig. 58. *Coprinus pellucidus*, habit and vertical section of cap cuticle.

Fig. 59. *C. pseudoradiatus*, habit and veil constituents.

Fig. 60. *C. vermiculifer*, habit and veil constituents.

Fig. 61. *C. filamentifer*, veil constituents.

Fig. 62. *C. stercoreus*, habit.

Fig. 63. *C. cordisporus*, vertical section of cap showing nature of veil cells on the cap cuticle.

Fig. 64. Veil cells with structural (l) and superficial crystalline (r) ornamentation.

22(21)	Cap without setules.	23
-	Cap with setules.	24

101

23(22)   Cap minute, 1-5mm high before expanding, reddish orange at first, soon fading. Basidiospores almost globose to triangular in one view, elliptic in another, 7-10 × 7-9 × 5.5-6.5μm. (2- and 4-spored forms have been found).

Coprinus miser

-   Cap larger, up to 15mm when expanded. Basidiospores pip-shaped, 7.5-8.5 × 9.5-11 × 9.5-11.5μm. (4-spored).

Coprinus nudiceps

24(22)   Spores hexagonal, 10-13 × 6.5-7.5μm. Cap purplish.

Coprinus hexagonosporus

-   Spores ellipsoid. Cap brown or reddish, without purplish tints.   25

25(24)   Basidia 4-spored.   26

-   Basidia 2-spored. Spores 11-13 × 5.5-7μm. Facial cystidia absent.

Coprinus bisporus

(*Coprinus sassii*, not yet recorded in British Isles, has 2-spored basidia with very large ellipsoid spores up to 20μm long).

26(25)   Cap with a mixture of hyaline and brown thick-walled setules. Spores 9-10 × 5.5-6μm, with eccentric germ pore. Facial cystidia absent.

Coprinus heterosetulosus

-   Cap with only one type of setule. Facial

cystidia present or absent.   27

27(26)   Facial cystidia present. Spores 7.9-13.3 ×
         4.4-6.4µm, with apical germ pore.
                                    Coprinus stellatus

-        Facial cystidia absent. Spores elongate and
         narrow, rarely greater than 5µm wide,
         with apical germ pore. Fruit body usually
         quite small, up to 6mm before expanding.
                              Coprinus pellucidus (fig. 58)
         (Several species in the group, e.g. *C.*
         congregatus and *C. ephemerus* have been
         found on straw/dung mixtures).

28(21)   Veil strongly adhering to cap. Spores
         elliptic ovate, 15-20 × 8-12µm. Stem with
         distinct ring. Usually on buried dung.
                                  Coprinus sterquilinus

-        Veil more floccose or powdery. Stem lacking
         ring or, if present (*C. ephemeroides*), fruit
         body small with 5-angled spores less than
         10µm long.   29

29(28)   Veil composed of filamentous units.   30

-        Filamentous units, if present, masked by a
         preponderance of rounded cells.   35

30(29)   Veil composed of strings of sausage-shaped,
         thin-walled, hyaline cells.   31

-        Veil composed of rather narrow, slightly
         thickened hyphae.   32

31(30)   Spores large, 11-14 × 6-7μm. Cap up to 1cm before expanding. Fruit body with or without a rooting base.

                                     Coprinus radiatus

-      Spores smaller, up to 9μm long. Cap up to 6mm before expanding. Fruit body without a rooting base.

                         Coprinus pseudoradiatus (fig. 59)

(*C. cinereus* is found on straw/dung mixture and *C. macrocephalus*, with large spores, has been recorded on raw dung).

32(30)   Veil citrus- or lime-yellow, or a mixture of hyaline and brown strongly coloured hyphae.   33

-      Veil grey or whitish.   34

33(32)   Veil of yellow hyphae. Spores 10.5-12.5 × 6-7.5μm.

                            Coprinus luteocephalus

-      Veil with brown hyphae. Spores 7-9 × 3.5-5μm.

                              Coprinus poliomallus

34(32)   Veil hyphae thin-walled. Spores 6.5-7.5 × 5μm, 'shouldered' about the apiculus.

                       Coprinus filamentifer (fig. 61)

-      Veil hyphae thin- and thick-walled, often with clamps. Spores elliptic-oblong, 9-10 × 5-6μm.

                       Coprinus vermiculifer (fig. 60)

(*Coprinus flocculosus*, with spores 11.5-16.5 × 6-9.5μm, can be found on straw/dung mixtures).

35(29) Stem with small, distinct ring. Spores subglobose to lentiform and 5-angled, 6-9 × 6.5-8 × 5-6μm.

Coprinus ephemeroides

\- Stem at most with fibrils, even then rarely forming a faint ring zone. 36

36(35) with setules in addition to veil. 37

\- Cap without setules. 38

37(36) Cap cystidia tapered. Spores 11-14 × 5-6.5μm.

Coprinus heptemerus

\- Cap cystidia capitate. Spores 10-11 × 6-7μm. *Coprinus curtus*

38(36) Veil of inflated bladder-like cells attached to filamentous units. Spores 7.5-8 × 4.5-5.5μm.

Coprinus utrifer

\- Veil of globose and subglobose cells and filamentous units often encrusted or with minute projections found sometimes at cap margin. 39

39(38) Globose cells, if ornamented then possessing crystalline or amorphous material (dissolved by 1N HCl, fig. 64.) 40

| - | Globose cells covered in small fine blunt projections on the walls (not removed by 1N HCl, fig. 64). | 45 |

| 40(39) | Basidia 2-spored. | 41 |
| - | Basidia 4-spored. | 42 |

| 41(40) | Spores 14-17 × 8.5-10 × 12.5-14μm. | *Coprinus pachyspermus* |
| - | Spores smaller, 9-11 × 6-6.5 × 8-9μm. | |

Coprinus cordisporus (2-spored form)

42(40) Spores less than 10μm long.

Coprinus cordisporus (fig. 63)
(*C. patouillardii* is known on garden refuse, and an undescribed species with lemon-shaped spores has recently been found).

- Spores 10μm or more long.   43

43(42) Veil soon discolouring greyish, drab or buff, Spores 11.5-14.5 × 6-8 × 7.5-9μm.

Coprinus cothurnatus

- Veil remaining snowy white, only slowly discolouring greyish.   44

44(43) Fruit bodies several cm tall. Spores 15-19 × 8.5-11.5 × 11-13μm.

Coprinus niveus

- Cap small, 5-6mm at first. Spores 14-16 x 8-9 × 10-12.5μm.

Coprinus latisporus

45(39)	Basidia 3-spored.	46
-	Basidia 4-spored.	47

46(45) Spores narrow, 8.5-11 × 5-6.2μm.   *Coprinus triplex*

- Spores broad, 9-10 x 6-6.5 × 6-7μm, slightly flattened in face view.

Coprinus trisporus

(These are possibly a single taxon).

47(45) Spores 7-8 × 4-4.5μm, perispore not visible in water or alkali mounts.

Coprinus stercoreus (fig. 62)

- Spores 9μm or more long.   48

48(47) Spores 9-11 × 5.5-6μm. Perisporal sac none or incomplete or indistinct.

Coprinus foetidellus

- Spores longer, 10.8-13.5 × 5.5-7μm, with distinct perispore with dark lines and inclusions. Distinctive smell of gas.

Coprinus narcoticus

(*C. sclerotiger* is found on straw/dung mixtures, and the smaller *C. tuberosus* on garden refuse etc.).

49(20) Spores not discoloured in conc. H_2SO_4.   50

- Spores discolouring in conc. H_2SO_4. Gills not spotted at maturity.   66

50(49)   Cap cuticle cellular. Gills spotted at
         maturity. (More often on rich, 'dungy',
         soils. *P. subbalteatus*, with copper coloured
         cap, drying paler but retaining a dark
         marginal zone, occurs in gardens on mulch
         etc.).
                                        (*Panaeolus*) 51

-        Cap cuticle filamentous.   56

51(50)   Velar remnants very obvious, either as an
         appendiculate veil or as a distinct ring.   52

-        Lacking all velar remnants.   54

52(51)   Cap distinctly pigmented, with
         appendiculate veil.   53

-        Cap pale coloured, smooth, semi-globate,
         soon cracking. Gills with marginal cystidia
         only.
                              Panaeolus papilionaceus

53(52)   Cap brown, smooth, sometimes viscid, not
         exceedingly wrinkled.
                               Panaeolus campanulatus

-        Cap grey, olivaceous, even black, with
         contrasting white appendiculate veil.
                                Panaeolus sphinctrinus

54(51)   Cap with or without appendiculate veil,
         but always with distinct ring.
                                 Panaeolus semiovatus

-        Cap lacking veil.   55

55(54) Cap pinkish ochraceous to tawny-buff.
        Lacking facial cystidia.

                                          Panaeolus speciosus

-       Cap whitish or slightly yellowish. With
        facial cystidia.

                                          Panaeolus antillarum

56(50) Gills with facial cystidia often containing
        yellow amorphous material when seen in
        ammonia solution or deep blue with cotton
        blue.

                                          (*Stropharia*) 57
        (Blue-green *S. cyanea* & *S. aeruginosa* often
        occur in rich garden soils).

-       Gills lacking facial cystidia. Never with
        yellowing cystidia in ammonia.

                                          (*Psilocybe*) 58
        (Red-capped *P. aurantia* can be found on
        straw/mulch mixtures in gardens).

57(56) Cap sticky, semi-globate ± expanding at
        maturity. On raw dung.

                                          Stropharia semiglobata

-       Cap plano-convex, often broad with a
        central umbo, margin flaring with age. On
        dungy mixtures in gardens.

                                          Stropharia stercoraria

58(56) Stipe bluing, with ring. Spores ellipsoid,
        11-14 × 6.5-7.5µm. Fruit body with mealy
        smell and taste.

Psilocybe fimetaria

- Stipe lacking distinct ring, or if with ring or ring zone 2-spored and/or stem not bluing. Fruit body without mealy smell and taste. 59

59(58) Stem always with distinct ring. Basidia 2-spored. Spores 15-20µm long.

Psilocybe luteonitens

- Stem with or without ring. Basidia 4-spored. If with ring, spores smaller. 60

60(59) With ring zone. 61

- Lacking velar remnants on stem, or only appendiculate teeth at cap margin. 62

61(60) Spores slightly angular/limoniform, 11-13(14) × 7-8µm. Often on sewage sludge.

Psilocybe merdaria

- Spores 13-14 × 7.5-8.5µm. *Psilocybe moelleri*

62(60) Spores 14-20 × 8-10µm. *Psilocybe subcoprophila*

- Spores smaller. 63

63(62) Spores lentiform, angled, 6-8(8.5) × 4.5-5.5 × 3.75-4.5µm.

Psilocybe bullacea

(*P. crobula*, occasional on dung, differs in lacking purple colour in gills, and slightly smaller, ovoid, not angular, spores).

-	Spores larger.	64
64(63)	Spores ellipsoid to slightly amygdaliform.	*Psilocybe merdicola*
-	Spores lentiform, angular.	65
65(64)	Spores 11-13(14) × 7-8(9)μm.	see *Psilocybe merdaria*, 61
-	Spores 12-15 × 8-9.5μm.	*Psilocybe coprophila*

66(49) Round cells on cap as a micaceous veil. (Re-examine gill face; if different sized basidia and facial cystidia separating the gills are present go to *Coprinus* at 21).

Psathyrella sphaerocystis

- Cap lacking veil, or if present then fibrillar. 67

67(66) White copious veil at margin or also covering cap centre. Spores 10-12 × 5.5-6μm.

Psathyrella coprobia

- Lacking copious veil. 68

68(67) With red edge to gill. Spores 12-13 × 6-6.5μm, with central germ pore.

Psathyrella stercoraria

- Lacking red gill edge. Spores with eccentric germ pore.

Psathyrella coprophila
(*P. fimetaria* differs in spore size; there are several members of the *P. prona* group which grow on soil/straw mixtures).

69(2)   Fruit body club-shaped.

                                                Typhula setipes (fig. 65)

          (*Clavaria acuta* often grows on peaty soil in pots in greenhouses).

-        Fruit bodies effuse, resupinate   70

70(69)   Fruit-body cobweb-like and greyish white. Basal hyphae 3-4.5μm wide. Spores sub-globose, 4.5μm diam. (Generally on old dung or straw/soil mixtures).

                                        Athelia coprophila

          (If with spiny spores 5-6μm diam., see the recently recorded *Tomentellopsis echinospora*).

-        Fruit-body with pores, white or flushed slightly ochraceous, brownish or greyish. (On clods of soil in dunged land).

                                        Cristella candidissima

71(1)   Fruit body either a cup containing several 'eggs' or a single orange or yellowish gelatinous sphere.   72

-        Fruit-body effuse, without distinct shape.   73

72(71)   Fruit-body whitish or pale yellow, up to 2.5mm diam., splitting at maturity to shoot away the orange/yellow spore mass.

                             Sphaerobolus stellatus (fig. 66)

-        Fruit-body cup shaped, with silvery-grey 'eggs'. (Usually on dung and straw or attached to rabbit pellets).

                                  Cyathus stercoreus

(*Cyathus vernicosus* often grows in plant pots on rich soil).

73(71)   Basidia with transverse septa. Spores 11 × 7μm. Fruit body pinkish.

Platygloea fimicola

(Not British; included for completeness. *Pilacrella solani*, with a glistening stipitate head, has been isolated from dungy soil).

-    Basidia with longitudinal septa. Spores 14-18 × 9-10μm. Fruit body cream-white or ivory.

Sebacina incrustans

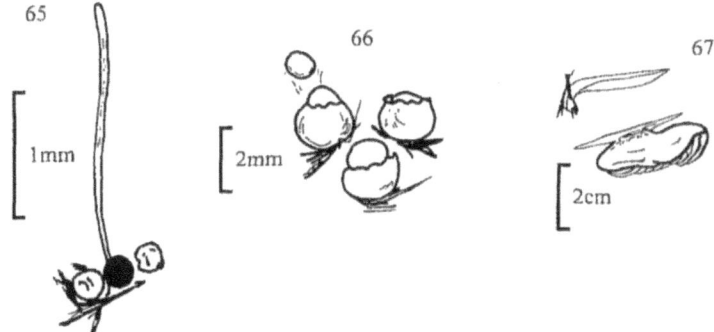

Fig. 65. Habit sketch of *Typhula* sp. Note attachment to sclerotium.
Fig. 66. *Sphaerobolus stellatus*, habit.
Fig. 67. *Clitopilus passackerianus*, a sessile agaric — habit sketch and section.

Key 4. Zygomycota

1   Spores formed in multispored sporangia (figs 68, 70, 72, 75, 76) or in few-spored sporangioles (figs 70, 73).   2

-    Multispored sporangia and globose

113

sporangioles absent. Spores formed singly on terminal, lateral or intermediate vesicles (figs 74, 79, 80, 82-86), or in short chains (figs 77, 78, 81). 11

2(1)   Sporangiophore stout, simple, with a subsporangial swelling and a basal swelling buried in the substrate. Sporangia tough walled, black, projected some distance towards the light when mature, and sticking to whatever they hit.

Pilobolus (fig. 76)

e.g. spores pale yellow, 8-10 × 5-6μm - *P. crystallinus*

spores orange, 12-20 × 6-10μm. - *P. kleinii*

-    Sporangiophores not stout; sporangia not violently discharged. 3

3(2)   Sporangial wall black, tough, not readily broken when touched. Sporangia with a sticky base, becoming attached to whatever they contact after the marked elongation of the white sporangiophores at maturity.

Pilaira (fig. 75)

e.g. spores yellowish, 8-10 × 6μm - *P. anomala*

spores colourless, 11-13 × 6-8μm - *P. moreaui*

-    Sporangial wall diffluent, spores readily removed in a droplet, or fragile and then spores easily dispersed by external violence. 4

4(3)   Sporangiophores stiff and metallic in

114

appearance, growing towards the light and
often to great length (5-30cm).

Phycomyces

e.g. spores 10.5-30 × 6.5-17μm;
columella pyriform; sporangiophores
up to 30cm - *P. nitens*
spores 8-13 × 5-7.5μm; columella
spherical or ovoid; sporangiophores *P.*
up to 30cm - *blakesleeanus*

\-   Sporangiophores white, not reaching
extreme lengths.   5

5(4) Small lateral sporangia (sporangioles)
present.   10

\-   Sporangioles absent.   6

6(5) Sporangiophores usually grouped, less often
single, connected by stolon-like hyphae.   7

\-   Sporangiophores arising singly, or if grouped
then lacking stolon-like hyphae.   9

7(6) Stolons joining groups of sporangiophores
often with rhizoids at the base of the group.   8

\-   Sporangiophores arising singly or in groups
from stolons, which may be 'rooted' at
intervals along their length, but rarely
beneath the groups of sporangiophores.

Absidia (fig. 71)

e.g. sporangiophores grouped,
rhizoids poorly developed; spores
2.5-4.5μm diam. - *A. corymbifera*
sporangiophores grouped, rhizoids

strongly developed; spores 2.5-
3.5µm diam. - *A. orchidis*

8(7)   Sporangiophores mostly unbranched.

Rhizopus (fig. 69)

e.g. spores irregularly angular-
ovoid, 8-14 × 11µm - *R. nigricans*

-    Sporangiophores with a whorl of branches beneath the main sporangium, each with a small columellate sporangium. Spores 6-8.5µm.

Actinomucor elegans

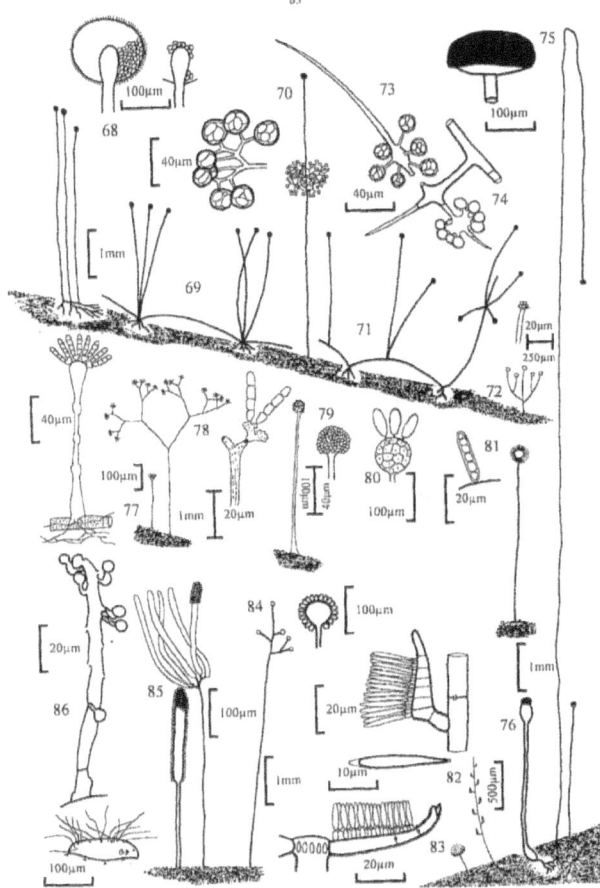

Fig. 68. *Mucor*, habit and detail of sporangium before and after dehiscence.

Fig. 69. *Rhizopus*, habit.

Fig. 70. *Thamnidium elegans*, habit and detail of sporangioles.

Fig. 71. *Absidia*, habit.

Fig. 72. *Mortierella*, habit and sporangiophore tip after sporangial dehiscence.

Fig. 73. *Helicostylum*, sporangioles.

Fig. 74. *Chaetocladium*, sporangioles.

Fig. 75. *Pilaira*, sporangiophores before and after elongation, and sporangium.

Fig. 76. *Pilobolus*, sporangiophore.

Fig. 77. *Syncephalis*, habit, sporangiophore and merosporangia.

117

Fig. 78. *Piptocephalis,* habit and detail of final branch with head cell and merosporangia.

Fig. 79. *Oedocephalum,* habit and sporing head.

Fig. 80. *Rhopalomyces,* sporing head.

Fig. 81. *Syncephalastrum,* habit and detail of merosporangium.

Fig. 82. *Coemansia,* habit, sporoclade with sporangia and sporangium with spore inside.

Fig. 83. *Kickxella,* habit and sporoclade.

Fig. 84. *Cunninghamella,* habit and fertile head.

Fig. 85. *Mycotypha* (l) and *Ostracoderma* (r) conidiophores.

Fig. 86. *Ballocephala,* habit of sporangiophores growing from parasitised tardigrade, sporangiophore and sporangia.

9(6)   Sporangia often with pigmented walls, yellowish when young, finally grey or black, with well marked columella left after spore dispersal. Individual sporangiophores observable with unaided eye, up to 20mm long.

Mucor (fig. 68)

e.g. spores smooth, 7-8 × 2.5-4.5μm - *M. hiemalis*

spores smooth, 6-12 x 3-6μm - *M. mucedo*

spores asperulate, 5-8.μm diam. - *M. plumbeus*

(N.B. *Zygorhynchus* would key out with *Mucor*. It is more often isolated from soil, and is distinguished from *Mucor* by the presence of zygospores with unequal suspensors)

-   Sporangia white, without a columella, readily becoming a spore droplet. Sporangiophores delicate, often only 200-400μm long. Fine, white, garlic-smelling mycelium often present.

Mortierella (fig. 72)

118

e.g. spores 16-27μm diam, few in
each sporangium;
sporangiophores *ca* 150μm, with
short lateral branches at right
angles - *M. reticulata*
spores 6-10 x 4-6μm;
sporangiophores 2-3mm high,
with ascending branches - *M. bainieri*
spores 4-10μm; sporangiophores
richly branched - *M. candelabrum*

10(5)   Sporangioles formed at the final tips of a
densely dichotomous system of branchlets,
originating some distance below a terminal
sporangium (which may be absent in young
specimens). Sporangioles up to 25μm diam.,
with up to 6 spores. Spores 8-12 × 6-8μm.
Thamnidium elegans (fig. 70)

-   Sporangioles either at the curved tips of
slender branches, or clustered in groups
about halfway along tapering branches
which radiate from the sporangiophore
below the sporangium; the branch tips of
the latter give the fertile portion of the
sporangiophore a bristly appearance.
Helicostylum (fig. 73)

e.g. spores 8-17 × 3-7μm;
sporangioles on short
secondary or tertiary branches;
fertile region bristly with sterile
branches - *H. fresenii*
spores 6-8 × 4μm; sporangioles
reflexed, on slender primary or
secondary branches; fertile

region without sterile branches
                                    - *H. pyriforme*

11(1)   Spores formed in chains.   12

-        Spores formed singly.   14

12(11)   Sporangiophores regularly and repeatedly
         dichotomously branched. Chains of 2-10
         spores produced in small groups, which
         may be wet or dry, on deciduous heads, 4-
         15μm diam. Parasitic on other fungi,
         mostly other Mucorales.
                              Piptocephalis (fig. 78)
                 e.g. spores 4-5 × 2-3μm, in
                         pairs; heads dry - *P. lepidula*
                 spores 5-6 × 2-2.5μm, in chains
                         of 4-9; heads dry - *P. cylindrospora*
                 spores 4-8 × 2-4μm, in chains of
                 3-5; heads dry; sporangiophore
                         without rhizoids - *P. freseniana*
                 spores 4-6 × 4-4.5μm, in chains
                         of 3-6; heads wet;
                 sporangiophore with rhizoids - *P. repens*
                 spores 3-5 × 2-2.5μm, in chains
                         of 3-5, heads wet; head cell
                 lyses, to leave only a fringe at
                         the tip of the very fine
                         sporangiophore - *P. fimbriata*

-        Sporangiophores simple or irregularly
         branched.   13

13(12)   A large conspicuous fungus,
         macroscopically Mucor-like, mycelium

coarse. Sporangiophores with a distinct terminal swelling with crowded spore chains. Spores usually 5-10 in a chain, globose to ovoid, 2-8 × 4-6μm.

Syncephalastrum racemosum (fig. 81)

\- Sporangiophores less conspicuous, 100-1000μm high, with a 'holdfast' at the base attaching the sporangiophore to the substrate. Mycelium very fine. Parasitic on other Mucorales.

Syncephalis (fig. 77)

e.g. sporangiophores 100-200μm high, with three 'nodes' along their length; merosporangia often forked at the basal cell; spores 8-10 × 6μm - *S. nodosa* sporangiophores up to 750μm high; merosporangia usually subdivided at their base into several branches, each with 5-10 spores; spores 5-10 × 3-4μm - *S. depressa* (N.B. *Oedocephalum* spp. (fig. 79), the anamorphic states of many dung fungi (esp. Ascobolaceae and Pezizaceae), *Rhopalomyces* (fig. 80), and some *Aspergillus* spp. are superficially similar to *Syncephalis* at first sight).

14(11) Sporangia containing a single closely fitting elongated spore, produced in serried ranks on one side of a boat-shaped branch (sporoclade). 15

\- Single-spored sporangia ('spores') globose,

produced singly or if in groups not on
sporoclades.   16

15(14)   Sporoclades lateral. Sporangiophores
         usually yellowish. (No parasitism has been
         demonstrated, but in culture grows much
         better in the presence of the white, garlic-
         smelling *Mortierella* spp.).

                              Coemansia (fig. 82)

             e.g. spores 6-11μm long;
            sporoclades spirally arranged
                 around the axis - *C. erecta*
      spores 16-18μm long; sporoclades
         formed on one side of the axis,
      causing it to curve to one side - *C. scorpoidea*

-        Sporoclades produced in a terminal verticil.
         Sporangiophores shining white.
                    Kickxella alabastrina (fig. 83)

16(14)   Spores produced in clusters below the apex
         of the final branches of a compound, often
         trifid, branching system which is given a
         bristly appearance by the projecting tips.
         Superficially similar to *Thamnidium* or
         Helicostylum. Capable of parasitising, and
         growing much better in association with,
         other Mucorales.
                         Chaetocladium (fig. 74)

            e.g. spores smooth, 4-6μm
                   diam. - *C. brefeldii*
       spores echinulate, 6.5-9.5μm - *C. jonesii*

-        'Spores' not produced in subterminal
         clusters, but terminally on lateral vesicles,

or over the surface of swollen fertile
regions of the sporangiophore.   17

17(16)   Sporangiophores up to 250μm high.
          Lateral vesicles numerous, each producing
          a single 'spore', which is projected when
          mature. Parasitic on tardigiades.
                                   Ballocephala (fig. 86)

-         Sporangiophores visible with the unaided
          eye. Spores produced on swollen parts of
          the sporangiophore.   18

18(17)   Sporangiophores branched, with more or
          less globose terminal fertile regions. Spores
          dry and powdery, yellowish or pinkish in
          mass.
                                   Cunninghamella (fig. 84)
          e.g. spores smooth, ovoid,
          18-22 × 10-14μm or globose,
                      8-10μm diam. - *C. elegans*
          spores echinulate, ovoid, 8-
                      12μm - *C. africana*

-         Sporangiophores unbranched, fertile
          portion 200-300 × 15-20μm. Fertile region
          terminal only, cylindrical. Spores smooth,
          greyish in mass, 2-4μm diam.
                           Mycotypha microspora (fig. 85)
          (N.B. *Ostracoderma epigea* (fig. 85), the
          anamorph of *Peziza astracoderma*, which
          occurs on paper and sometimes dung and
          highly organic substrates, was originally
          described as *Mycotypha dichotoma*. The fertile
          regions are cylindrical but multiple as the

result of several close dichotomous
divisions at the base of the fertile portion).

Notes

[1]

There are few reports of *Ascozonus*, apart from *A. woolhopensis*. Observed spore sizes of *A. woolhopensis* suggest that measurement of Renny's (1874) illustrations of spores leads to values which are too large (19-20 × 6-6.5µm). Those in parentheses are what they might be, based on the discrepancy between observed values for *A. woolhopensis* and Renny's illustration.

www.ingramcontent.com/pod-product-compliance
Lightning Source LLC
Chambersburg PA
CBHW032017010726

47493CB00007B/2449